HEAR ME

Praise for Hear Me:

SKYE WARREN

CONTENTS

AUTHOR'S FOREWORD

Dear reader,

It seems that the warnings for my books have wavered between barely there and too dire, so I'll share with you my thoughts on dark erotica. I write about pain the way a paranormal author writes magic: early and often. There is torture and sex, sometimes in the same breath. This is a fantasy for those who like it when it hurts. If that is you, I hope you'll come along for the ride.

Many thanks to Leila DeSint, K.M., Bibliopolist, Em Petrova, Helen Hardt and Emily Eva Heatherington for making this book possible.

Skye Warren

SKYE WARREN

CHAPTER ONE

Even the earth conspired to keep her. Branches grabbed at her skin like talons; the beach was quicksand, dragging her down. Hope was too abstract to compete with the sound of men shouting behind her. Even her fear was drowned by the ragged beat of her heart.

"Melody!" The voice sounded closer than the thrashing of leaves and branches.

Run, run away, don't look back.

Her eyes, already stunted by lack of food, filled with grit and precious moisture. If she made it to the water, she could float away. Even if only to drift down to the bottom, entombed in sand castles and chained by seaweed. They would take her prisoner; they would keep her safe.

A battered person was cracked soil, but dreams were like weeds. She could survive this. That was the goal she set for herself, huddled in the cold, damp cell. She had clung to it as they touched her, beat her. Trained her.

The line of frothy water was in her sights but disappointment seared her. She was too far away, the sand too thick.

An extra burst of energy propelled her two more stumbling steps. Her legs gave out. She clenched and released fistfuls of sand, not even sure she was actually crawling forward.

Coolness lapped at her fingertips, surprising her. Her mind, tired and rusty, turned that information over. She had made it. Water. Safety? No, freedom.

A slow, steady *thwapping* noise drew her gaze upward. A small green boat bobbed in the shallow water. Gentle waves flicked its hull, almost soothing, like the caress of a flogger. The rhythm thrummed through her. Even without the sting of impact, her mind began the slide.

No. Subspace meant security but not today. Right now it meant death, and she refused to die.

She blinked away the salt in her eyes and clawed through the water to the boat. With a strength that surprised her, she climbed over the edge, tumbling into the grimy bottom. It rocked gently with her weight then settled back into the gentle bob.

The boat wasn't tied down anywhere, but there wasn't an oar. Not that she had the strength to use one or a place to go.

Never mind. Her wish had been granted. She would drift out to sea, like a message in a bottle.

Her head lolled against the rim of the boat. She breathed in the pungent smell of earth and moss. Her last thought before she drifted off to sleep was fanciful. She imagined a giant plucking her from the water, unfurling her like a scroll, and reading the lines slashed into her skin.

She wondered what they would say.

Awareness washed over her, sending a small thrill through her sated limbs. There was always a sense of achievement in waking up, in knowing she'd lived through another day. She allowed herself a portion of pride. She had beaten them for one day more.

Of course, the morning was always the high point.

Every day it was the same. Bruises upon bruises. Welts upon welts. Everything ached, even now, but she knew better than to move. It wouldn't make her feel better, and there was always the chance it would draw their attention. Anything was better than that, including lying unnaturally still on cold, damp concrete.

Except it didn't feel all that cold or damp. It was hard to register anything above the agony in her muscles, but she felt something like cloth against her fingertips. She brushed it again, the softness foreign but seductive. Despite her worry and her hurt, she felt warm. Protected.

Instead of forcing herself into rigid stillness, she was relaxed.

A whiff of something like fresh morning air tickled her nose. That couldn't be right. The ventilation from the small barred window high in her cell never competed with the stench of sweat and blood and fear. But there was the unmistakable smell of fresh, yeasty bread. Her mouth watered.

Her eyelids felt like they were weighted down with buckets of sand; she pried them open. Whiteness surrounded her. Not good. Loss of vision was one of the side effects of starvation. The slave in the cell next to hers couldn't see anything for two days before she died.

Maybe she was about to die, and that was why she was hallucinating food and seeing clean white where gray and mold and pain should have been. It should have been terrifying to find herself on the brink of what she'd fought for so long. Instead, the blankness soothed her. The smells made her mouth water.

She didn't want to die, but this didn't feel like death.

The edges of her sight sharpened, and her mind put names on her surroundings. Whitewashed walls instead of metal bars. A bed beneath her instead of a flea-ridden pallet.

She recognized none of it, but the sweetness of it all acted as a drug in her veins, keeping her from panicking. *Safe*, she thought, even though she had no reason to know they wouldn't hurt her here too. *Home*, she thought, even though she was sure she'd never seen it before.

Curiosity nudged at her until she lifted the sheet. Clothes! Well, maybe that was too strong a word for the soft worn shirt that draped her body and stopped mid-thigh. Her memory was hazy, limited at best, but clothes were new, she was sure of that much.

The sight of her torn and mottled skin tainted the daydream. And the pain rang true.

She peeled back the soft fabric to inspect her body.

There were the usual marks, crisscrosses down her back and thighs she could feel with her fingertips, torn skin where the restraints cut into her wrists. There were new cuts too, but these didn't look like the ones from a whip. Uneven scratches all down the front of her body.

Scuff sounds on the wood floors grew louder, her only warning before a looming figure filled the doorway. For one terrifying moment, her mind translated the image of his thickly muscled form and scowling face into a childish nightmare. A monster come to get her because she'd left her foot hanging over the side of the bed.

Then reality snapped her back. Not a monster, not exactly. A master.

Her training kicked in. It didn't matter how she had ended up here in this strange, comfortable room at the mercy of this strange, sinister-looking master. She knew what to do. Her limp body slid from the bed and dropped to its knees. The movement awakened a thousand new aches, but it couldn't be helped. She bowed low, praying she looked properly worshipful.

The threat of danger prickled her entire body, set her hair on end, but the fight or flight response had been beaten right out of her. Either reaction could get her killed, or more likely, hurt so badly that death would be preferable. So she waited on the floor, letting the cool knotted wood bruise her knees, her arms, her forehead.

She waited for an order, because that was what she'd been taught to do in the presence of a master. No command came, and the air tingled with expectancy.

As the seconds ticked away, anxiety rose. Should she

do something, try a new position or ask how to please him? But any variation from her pose would be punished, she knew that.

The booted feet approached. Boots humiliated – they hurt. She held still, accepting. Probably she had done it wrong. Her heart sped up, but she fought the instinct to cringe away, to cover her head and vital organs, to beg for mercy. The pain of a kick echoed through her body, and he hadn't even touched her yet.

Large hands clamped beneath her arms, hauling her up. He tossed her onto the bed, where she landed in an ungainly sprawl.

Even terrified, she kept her gaze lowered. Never look them in the eyes.

But he wasn't saying anything, and she'd already done one wrong thing. Once was a mistake. Any more would be considered willful disobedience. What did he want her to do?

She slowly looked up, already berating herself for the audacity.

Thick eyebrows made harsh lines across his face. His skin was tan and peppered with an uneven beard, as if it had been scraped at with an old blade by an impatient hand.

How long had it been since she looked directly at another person?

The long raised scar down his cheek shocked her. *Only human*, it said. But the cold cast of his eyes disabused her of that notion quickly. No understanding, no trace of pity. Uncontrollable shivers racked her body.

Impossibly, he frowned further.

She was an idiot. God, she knew better than to look directly at him, to show her fear without prompting. Hadn't they taught her? Over and over again. The memories flashed.

She needed to show him that she hadn't meant it as defiance. He wanted her on the bed, that much was clear, but based on his tacit displeasure, he wanted something else from her. She couldn't ask, not without making everything worse. Her mind scrabbled desperately for some way to show her deference, her subservience, without words. Knowing it would fail but desperate, she bowed again atop the rumpled sheets.

Rough hands tightened on her arms once more and flung her back against the pillows.

"Stop that." His voice rumbled through, over her.

She relaxed her body across the bed. Let him do with her what he would. Sex, violence. Her mind reached for that faraway place where none of this mattered. Where none of it was really happening anyway.

But when he put his thick hand on her ankle, panic rose like bile.

There had never been a more innocent place to touch her than her ankle, and the light pressure was more of a caress than anything, but it hit her like a slap. Her leg jerked, shaking his hand off of her. She stared in horror at her mutinous leg, shocked that she could ever do something so stupid.

The insults of her Masters played in her head. Disobedient slut. Willful little cunt. Worthless whore. God, she would deserve every lash he meted out.

"Stay," he said then left the room.

Gone to get something to hit her with, ties to hold her down, probably. Pain awaited her, that message rang clearly in every stark plane of his face and thick muscle banding his body.

She had precious seconds alone with which to get her bearings. The last thing she remembered was being asleep in her cell. There had been extra activity for the past couple of days. While she got her daily whipping, one of her Masters had talked to another.

Who do you think's going to get her?

Some rich fuck. Lucky bastard too. This one takes it like a dream.

They all do, tied down like that.

She's quiet. The rest of them make a fucking racket. I hear the goddamned screams in my sleep.

She had been sold. The realization settled into her stomach with dread and resignation. That was what they were talking about. Wondering who would buy her.

The thought of leaving her cell terrified her, but it was already done. She couldn't remember the transport, but that was probably just as well. She assumed it wouldn't be pleasant, but then, she couldn't remember her arrival at the compound either. All she knew was training.

At some point, her previous life had slipped away from her, like an old skin that no longer fit. She knew better than to try to remember. If whatever she had known or believed before threatened her survival in this life, she was better off without it.

The women who clung to their old identities suffered more. They fought until their last breath, finally mastered by their own stubbornness. What was the cost of sucking a cock or licking a boot when compared to life? No, she wanted to survive.

The men had whips and restraints. The only weapon she had was utter obedience.

Another thought occurred to her. Maybe they had given her something to knock her out or tamper with her memory. Gratitude welled inside her. They always took care of her. Sometimes it hurt, but she surely deserved it. Every lash to her skin raised a mirroring lash of self-recrimination and guilt.

The doorframe gaped, empty. Her Master had been gone a long time now.

The thought of his return terrified her, but the alternative was even worse. Maybe she was too much trouble for him, and he wouldn't want her anymore. What if he wasn't getting some painful implement to punish her? What if he was contacting her old Masters at the compound, demanding they take her back?

Her stomach clenched painfully. She didn't know him, whether he would be cruel or merciful, but if she were returned to her old Masters, they would kill her.

She had barely made it through some of the harsher beatings. It was one of the reasons she was always obedient from early on. There wasn't a lot of rope in her to begin with, she couldn't afford for the Masters to burn through it.

She wanted to live. That had become her mantra, something she repeated to remind herself. Or maybe to convince herself that it was still true. On the bad days she felt like a ghost, going through the motions long after her death because she refused to accept it.

Thuds on the floorboards signaled the return of her Master.

He didn't have a cane or whip with him, and that lent credence to the worry that he was getting rid of her, but she was too distracted by the food. He carried a glass of water and a plate with fragrant bread. Her stomach grumbled. She cringed in fear of reprisal and a small amount of embarrassment.

He set the plate down in front of her and pushed the glass into her hands. "Drink."

It seemed unbearably luxurious, compared to the greasy scraps she was accustomed to. This room too, with its plain wood furniture and open window. Her new cage, gilded with cleanliness. She ached to keep it.

The cool water soothed her, revived her. He replaced the empty glass with a chunk of warm, crusty bread. She gobbled it up like the ravening animal she was. He tore off another piece from the plate and handed it to her, continuing to feed her from his hand until the plate was empty.

Warmth settled in her core and spread to her limbs, sated by both the sustenance and his kindness. No dog bowl held fetid water. No mealy scraps picked off the floor. Charity like this was unheard of, but she thought she understood the message. If she pleased him, this could be hers.

Whatever he wanted, she would do. She would have done it anyway, because he was her Master. She paid her keep with obedience. She might earn reprieve from the pain with obeisance. But this generosity came freely, and gratitude suffused her. Maybe he liked her.

"What's your name?" he asked.

Her heart sank. They must not have told him about her. So much for pleasing him.

Bracing herself, she slowly shook her head.

He grasped her chin and raised her head. Prompted by his touch, she raised her gaze to meet his. His eyes flickered, as if a dam barely leashed something within.

She flinched.

His fingers tightened, not enough to bruise. "Tell me."

Her mouth worked, but nothing came out. Nothing ever came out.

She couldn't remember her name, but that wasn't the problem. She could have told him that it was "slave," or if she could manage without sounding precocious, asked him what he wanted it to be. She could have explained that she couldn't remember anything before her captivity.

The real problem was she couldn't talk.

He sighed. "Do you have someone I can call?"

Oh God, he really was sending her back. The ultimate failure as a slave—rejection—and she'd managed to achieve it within an hour.

No. She would never survive the punishment. And besides, she liked this Master with his gentle touch and cozy bed. It was presumptuous to think she had a choice, blasphemous even, but there it was.

For as long as she could remember, which albeit wasn't long, she had wanted to be owned. Not in the compound amid the huddle of slaves and litany of

11

trainers but by one Master. Now she stood on a precipice between a generic slave and one with hope. She wanted *this* Master.

She flipped through the ways she knew to please and placate, all of them sexual. Her body was torn to bits, not pretty or sexy right now, if it ever was. She had no feminine wiles – none. Her body was too skinny, all the trainers berated her for it. Scrawny, weak.

In a reckless burst of courage, she reached out and put her hand directly on his cock. At first it felt like nothing, just the flat stiffness of his jeans. But then, *there*, it jumped beneath her palm, lengthened.

This was solid ground. She could arouse him, then she would get him off. Any way he wanted it, she had probably done it before, or she could learn. He would see her value then. It wasn't exactly obedient to grope your Master without express orders to do so. The opposite, really, but she was desperate.

He put his hand on the top of her head, not pushing her closer or away. It was sweet, his hesitation, and she thought for a moment that he would let her get away with it. God, she would do anything. *Please.*

He gently pushed her hand away.

She wanted to live. How pathetic.

Tears fell in hot tracks down her cheeks.

"Someone really did a number on you, didn't they?" he asked.

At his words, she looked into his eyes. Amazingly, they were filled with something like understanding. It was probably better that she couldn't speak then, because she would have begged for him to help her. But she didn't deserve his benediction. She'd failed.

"Here's what we're going to do." He slid his hand around her neck, grasping her firmly from behind. She melted into the firm touch. "You're going to sleep now. Stay off the floor. Nod for me."

She nodded vigorously, her eyes downcast in joy.

His fingers still curled behind her neck, he swept his thumb along her cheek, then down over her neck. Back and forth, he caressed her. She stayed still, watching as her breath ruffled the dark hairs on his forearm.

He moved his thumb against her mouth then pushed it inside. She closed her lips around it, eager to suck it. He tasted of salt and earth and hope. This was her chance to touch him, to please him, to show him badly she wanted this.

She swirled her tongue around the tip, worshipping his thumb like she wanted to worship his cock. Like she wanted to lick every part of him, if it meant she could stay. The soft wet sounds filled the room, tangling with the harsh sounds of his breathing.

She begged with the warmth and wetness of her mouth. She implored with the skill of her tongue. Every swipe promised pleasure, if only.

He pulled his hand away.

Her lips were still parted, damp from his ministrations. She stayed perched on the bed in supplication. A bulge rounded his jeans. His nostrils flared with what she recognized as arousal.

He turned and left the room.

She stared at the door for what felt like hours, until her limbs ached and her eyelids grew heavy. No trick.

She sank into the clean bed.

She caught the slight sound of crickets outside, serenading her under the window. He had been surprised to learn about her defect, but he had worked around it. *Nod for me.* Maybe he would keep her after all.

CHAPTER TWO

She had been naked before, cold before, but not like this. The chill bit into her skin, penetrated her bones, until she couldn't imagine ever being warm again. Stripped not just of clothes, but of humanity, of hope.

The dream, she was in it again. Dear God, *no. Get out. Wake up!*

The shadowy Masters in the dream paid no attention to her silent plea, just as they hadn't in her memory. The wet cloth covered her face, heavy and stifling. Panicked, she sucked in a breath. No, wrong, stupid, because her mouth filled with water, not air. There was no air, none. Not in her lungs, not in her nose. Only water, never-ending water in her face and all around.

Her whole body bucked with the effort to breathe, but all she earned was a brief respite, just the flash of distraction as the bonds cut into her wrists and ankles and neck. Then she was drowning. This time they had gone too far. No air – she gulped. She sucked the water into her lungs, knowing it was over. Hope faded, everything dimmed.

The rush of air shocked her before the bright lights could register. She drank in the air, free from the torture chamber of simple damp cloth.

Her face was wet, leftover water, but also with her tears, with snot, with drool. And lower too, she had wet herself, but she couldn't bring herself to embarrassment just yet. She couldn't control them, not a single one of her reactions, as her body spasmed and shook and grunted out primal sounds of relief and fear.

The master crossed his arms, angry, but his eyes were amused. "Don't have anything to say now, do you?"

Her body jerked in its restraints, though she couldn't have said why. Actually, she couldn't say anything. Her throat was frozen. Her mind pulled it to a halt like some large, clumsy piece of machinery now rutted into the dry ground. Good. She couldn't remember what she had said, but she thought she must have talked back. She must have mouthed off, and her masters didn't tolerate that.

"Answer me," he said.

What was the question? No, she had nothing to say him, not ever again if it meant she did not have to endure that again. Her body jerked and secreted fear in the form of bodily excretions, but it would eventually find equilibrium. But her mind—God. Her mind was numb, *waiting*, like that moment after seeing your thumb hit with a hammer but before the pain sets in. She would never be the same again. She would never be warm, never be safe again.

He flicked her, right on her forehead. "Cat got your tongue?"

She closed her eyes, opened them. Licked her lips and tried to speak, but nothing came out.

His eyebrow raised. "The correct answer is 'Yes, Master.'"

When nothing came out, he turned purple, splotchy. "You would disobey me now? That wasn't enough for you? Answer me, slave. *Say it.*"

Fear shuddered through her. Her throat worked, fruitless. She formed the words with her mouth, desperate. *Yes, Master, Yes, Master, Yesssssmaster.*

Her lips kept moving, even as the wet cloth clamped down on them. The water slapped her face, fell into her mouth, and blocked her nose. Only one lungful of air left. She opened her mouth to scream. Use it all up to scream, but it turned into a gargle. She gasped and gasped, breathing in water. Drowning, sinking, falling too deep to ever make her way back up in time.

She woke gasping for air, shivering. That nightmare again. *God.*

At least she couldn't remember it. That was a small comfort, but the effects on her body were chilling enough. It took her a minute to realize where she was again. Not her cell. She had a new master, one who kept a beautiful cell for her. One who fed her fresh bread and clean water.

It took her a moment to hear it: something between a groan and a whimper. She glanced at the window first, fearful of wild animals. The house was practically in the middle of a jungle. The sound came again, this time more clearly through the wall—from *inside* the house. When it was accompanied by a muted thump, she thought she knew what it was. Who it was.

Her feet hit the cold, gnarled wood, and she padded into the hallway silently. His door was open. She saw a shadowed figure flail on the bed, but far from scary, the sight was endearing. He had nightmares—like her.

She crept inside. How exactly would she wake him up without speech? Perhaps she could shake him, though the thought of touching him without permission... but she had to try. She knew the pain of being trapped inside a dream, again and again.

When she reached the side of the bed, he stilled. This room was darker than hers, without a window. The sheets drew gray relief against the black night. Perhaps his dream had ended.

In a flash of shadows and whip of wind, she was wrenched onto the bed. With a silent cry, she fell— caught by softness and blanketed with male musk. Uncertainty kept her still, but curiously she felt no fear.

No menace simmered in the air, just pain, and that was an old friend to her. Harsh breathing sawed just above her, touching her face like a caress. She waited, wanting. Longing for something, but what?

His hand on her breast, heavy and possessive, came as a shock. She jumped and twisted away. He didn't slap her for her error, only straightened her body out, pulled at her lips like she was nothing more than a cloth to be spread out nice and straight. But he knew what she was—flesh and blood, oh yes. His cock lay thick and hot against her thigh, burning, seeking. His hand returned to her breast, probing, tweaking.

She had been in the dark before—blindfolded, hurt. She had been touched by hands and cocks before— humiliated, used. But not like this. Tears stung her eyes. Long dormant arousal unfurled inside her. Blasphemous thoughts whispered through her: *you're not a slave. You're a woman.*

"I've missed you." His voice was hoarse, as if he'd been the one covered in a cloth and poured with water. A warm-cold touch on her nipple told her he'd licked her. "God, I've missed you so much."

This wasn't for her. Not his arousal, not his tenderness. It was for some woman in his memories.

Of course it had been too much to hope that she deserved it. He didn't even know her. She had done nothing to prove her service, to please him. But a part of her shriveled and fell away, and only then did she realize how much she wished for this. Only when it extinguished did she recognize the hope she had harbored all this time.

What did it matter if she was a good slave? What sort of goal was that?

She did the unthinkable: she pushed him away. It was nothing more than a nudge, her weak arms against a broad, unmovable chest. He caught her wrists and held them above her head, set her defiance aside as if it were nothing. *She* was nothing.

She lay still, unblinking at the night. Tiny specs floated across her vision—insignificant, like her. Her hands were pinned above her, her legs spread by his hips, but she wouldn't fight this.

He returned to her nipples, licking, suckling. It was instinctive, those actions, not a sign of affection. But the kisses—oh, they were different. His lips brushed the underside of her breast. He kissed the side and the sloping top, and then his lips met her chest in the middle, where her heart would be. He roamed higher, to her neck, and she felt her pulse beat against his lips. She swallowed. This would never be for her. Even the best slave didn't deserve such treatment.

Please. Her lips formed the words. No sound broke the silence, because she was a part of the night. A silent specter to complete his dream, a shadow of the woman he wanted.

She felt him nudge her entrance, the head of his cock broad and insistent. Instinctively she clenched, fearing the pain. He thrust inside—hard. She gasped.

"Oh Jesus. So *fucking* tight." He sounded drugged, still trapped in the dream that made this all okay. She knew all about that dream, the one with white lies and endless reasonings. Or with none at all: just live.

He pulled out and slammed back in, his cock reaching deep, and his thighs opening her wide. Her mouth was open, in shock, in pain. Although, it wasn't really pain. She was wet, at least, and he hadn't even needed lube. He was just big, and she had always been small.

Then his hips dipped, and he thrust upward, hitting a spot that made her eyes roll back in her head. She thrust her hips to meet him, like a slut, she was a slut, who cared when it felt like this? That awkward pain of betrayal faded beneath the onslaught of physical sensation. Her cunt ached, *she* ached, and then he moved harder, faster. She was pinned to the bed, and it seemed like he would never stop, and she didn't want him to.

But then he did. He pulled out, leaving her inner muscles clenching at nothing. With a smooth motion, he flipped her onto her stomach. She immediately tilted her hips up and back to meet him; he slipped inside. His body fit to hers, chest to her back and muscled thighs coarse against her own.

Making love.

The thought blinded her, streaking through her haze of sex and fear like a shooting star. That's what he was doing: making love to her. Even if it wasn't really her, it was beautiful. Even if he couldn't even see her in the dark, she *felt* beautiful.

"But why?" he whispered. "Why did you do it?"

A sharp slap to her ass shocked her. She grasped the sheet and waited for another, but it didn't come. His hand snaked around her body to cup her breasts, to pinch her nipples. And then twist. This time she felt her inner muscles spasm around his cock, and he groaned in her ear. That's what he was doing. Increasing his pleasure with her pain. Playing her body like an instrument, tuning it to sing for him.

She was still full of gladness for his earlier tenderness, and now a shroud of submission descended upon her. He pinched her other nipple, and she contracted again. She lifted her upper body ever so slightly to allow him better access. His breath caught, and then he sat up, pulling her up as well.

She sat up in the middle of a strange bed, in the dark, impaled on the cock of this Master she didn't know. He pulled and twisted her nipples, forcing her body to writhe in his cruel embrace. Her slavery had never been sweeter.

More. She wanted to do more for him. To please him in whatever way she could. She slid her hand down past where they were joined, hot and slippery, and farther. The soft skin of his sac was wet with their juices, and she stroked him there. Cupped and rolled his balls in her palm. His low moan was all the gratitude she could want. The way he slowed his thrusts to allow her better access was her order to continue. But when he softened his hold on her nipples, she faltered. Mercy always came with a price.

With heavy palms on her back, he tipped her forward. Her shoulders hugged the bed, leaving her ass completely exposed to his thrusts. He reached inside her, and now there was pain. Small twinges each time he struck deeply that left her breathless.

Every thrust came with a sound now, a grunt as the air left him in a rush. A groan that made her tighten around him as much as his pinches earlier had done. His fingers dug into the flesh of her hips, holding her steady even though she would never try to end this. But it was beyond her now, to fight or to please him, to do anything at all except take it. It had never been up to her; it would always come to this. Trapped under his weight, impaled with his cock, dripping in his sweat.

Isn't this what she wanted? So why was the sheet beneath her face wet? Why was the blackness blurry with her tears?

Take me. Use me. Want me. Oh God, somebody want me. I don't want to be worthless anymore.

"Fuck," he shouted, and the sound was like a gunshot in the night. It startled her, even as the thick pulse of his cock soothed her, familiar and warm. She clenched her eyes shut as his fingers dug rivers into her skin, as he groaned out his passion for some other woman into her body.

He collapsed beside her. She lay unmoving in that ignominious position, her ass in the air, her cunt dripping with his leavings, but there was no one to see her. No one to care. From tiredness or hopelessness her body slid down, straightened on the sheet, and she fell asleep in the puddle of salty fluids.

She hung from vines, tacked to the mossy wall by their thorns. The man with dark hair and dark eyes held no weapons, but his eyes held a knowledge of pain given and pleasure received.

"What do you want, girl?" he asked.

"Please let me down," she answered, and that's when she knew it was a dream.

He stroked her breast, pinched her nipple. Twisted. Oh, he liked that. "Try again."

"I want to be free," she said, meaning it this time.

Still, he shook his head.

This time he stuck two fingers inside her—three. It

burned and stretched and throbbed in confused arousal. "You're already wet," he said, holding up his fingers to show her. "What do you really want?"

She looked into his eyes and tasted his fear. He thought he needed vines to keep her. "If you let me go, I'll stay with you."

And so he let her down, each thorn leaving clean, bare skin as it was removed. Gladness beat in her breast. He'd trusted her, and now they could be together without chains. But then he was holding his belt, folded over.

"Come and kneel in front of me," he said, his voice soft and beguiling. "This is what you wanted."

She did it, embraced the pebbles and twigs that carpeted the ground. The belt seared into her back, and she gasped. Again; she arched and choked out a cry. Eventually she wailed, until she couldn't take it anymore.

She looked back. "Oh God. Please!"

His eyes were bright with bloodshed. *What do you want?*

This.

She woke to rustling behind her. The room wasn't overly bright now but enough to see by. The sense of accomplishment that usually met each day was marred by her dream. She tried to recapture the feeling, but it slipped away like her memories. Blinking away the sense of loss, she rolled over to face her Master.

He stared at her, a sea in storm. "You," he breathed.

She swallowed hard, lowering her eyes. He deserved her submission, but she would not feel guilty for what he had done to her. No matter how his tone sounded like an accusation. No matter the pain she saw marring his eyes.

From the corner of her vision, she saw his jaw clench. "Get the hell out of my bed."

CHAPTER THREE

She tentatively approached the kitchen, reluctant to make her presence known after his anger this morning. He had barely spoken to her since then, just directing her to the bathroom to wash up and handing over a thin yellow dress for her to wear. She didn't know where he'd gotten it.

In the kitchen, he was flipping eggs in a sizzling frying pan. He turned and stopped at the sight of her. After a beat, he gestured to the table. "Sit."

The plain chair was strangely comfortable, as if it conformed to her body even though that was impossible. And soft—the wood felt like velvet. This house and its furnishing were sparse, primitive even. But also cozy. Everything in its place.

Except for her.

He set a plate down in front of her with a large helping of scrambled eggs and bacon. She stared at the food. Her mouth watered, but her stomach turned. This rich food was a sharp contrast to the bland meal she was used to. She couldn't eat it, but neither could she rebuff such generosity.

Turning a chair around so that its back faced the table, he straddled it and dug into his own plate. For a moment, she was able to observe him without his returned regard. Black hair that looked softer by morning night. More tousled than unkempt. His features were definitely coarse—a bit too large for his face—but they suited his presence. Too much, exactly right.

Suddenly he looked up; her mouth went dry. His eyes were exactly as she remembered them: black, bottomless, and terrifying. It was just as well she couldn't see him last night. Those eyes would have seen too much.

"Aren't you going to eat?"

Gingerly, she picked up the fork. How long had it been since she held one?

He cocked his head, watching her as if she were a curious experiment. She tightened her fingers and stabbed a piece of egg. The tines made a loud ringing sound against the plate, and she winced.

She put the whole thing in her mouth and set the fork back down. The egg was thick and creamy and so foreign. It coated her tongue, and she forced a breath through her nose. God, she had swallowed so much worse than this—why not this? But she couldn't. *Get it out.*

And then a hand was over her mouth, not tightly just a touch. A stroke down her back, calming her. "Take it easy," he said. "Swallow it. There you go."

When she had gulped it down, he returned to his seat as if nothing had happened.

She blinked the tears from her eyes and stared down at the food in dismay. It was three times what she normally was fed. Did he expect her to eat the whole thing? She would throw it up. And then what would he do to her?

A scrape of the chair against the wood floor drew her attention to him. He put the chair beside hers and sank. Her eyes widened; his were dark and forbidding. It was too much, all of it: the food, his presence.

"Half," he said.

She blinked.

"We may not get through all of it today, but you'll eat half of what's on the plate. We'll work up to the rest another day. Deal?"

This was a negotiation? Of course, she couldn't actually say anything back so admittedly her bargaining position was poor, but she wasn't used to being asked for her opinion. She wasn't used to giving it. She frowned.

"I'm going to take that as a yes," he said, spearing another piece of egg.

At the touch of the food to her lips, her mouth opened. It was trained into her, and she swallowed.

"Good girl."

She ate two more bites before fidgeting. Already she felt full, so full. Normally her discomfort wouldn't matter, but something was different now. Strange and exciting. She wasn't saying no exactly, but she didn't want this.

The egg touched her lips, and she parted, only slightly. He raised his eyebrow.

Quickly she ate, strangely deflated. Her streak of rebellion was very small, but it didn't go unnoticed. He paused, examining her. Her heart raced in anticipation. Would he punish her now—or later? She almost wanted it. At least then she would know what to expect from him. At least then this confusing charade of normalcy would come to an end.

His large hands closed around her arms, and she winced. But no pain came. Instead she was enfolded in warmth—surrounded. She sat on his lap, held by him, fed by him, and she ate. If she paused or floundered, he would rub her back in slow circles. His touch was calm but sure. *I'll make you feel better*, it said, *but you'll still do what I say*.

But strangely, she found it easier to eat like this. Maybe because she could feel the steady beat of his heart and knew he wasn't angry at her. Maybe because his warmth and strength were used to shield her, not hurt her.

More than that, he seemed to recognize when she needed a moment, and he gave it to her. He was reading her cues, she realized. It was amazing; it was beautiful. Terrifying. He could hurt her so much worse than the others. He seemed to know what she was thinking even without her words. He knew what she was feeling. And hadn't she stopped talking to protect herself from such a thing?

No, that wasn't right. She didn't stop talking, she

couldn't speak. She had never spoken. It was just easier that way. Best not to think about it.

"What's going on in that head of yours?" he asked with a tap to her nose.

Her gaze snapped to him and then away, as if he *could* see.

He sighed and set the fork down. "I'm thinking of calling the Coast Guard. They ought to be able to pick you up, drop you off at the mainland."

She tensed all over, broke out into a sweat. The mainland. Where was that? Who would take care of her there? No, she didn't want that. She had angered him, but how? He'd been upset after last night, but he had still fed her after that. It was only when she couldn't speak that he wanted to send her away. Stupid slave. Broken slave.

But she could still please him. How to show it? She shook her head, just a quick shake.

"No?" he asked.

Clumsily, she took his hand in both of hers and brought it to her neck. Wrapped it around herself. His grip firmed for just a moment before his hand fell away.

"No," he repeated. "I know what you are. I know what you want. But I don't do that."

Anymore remained unspoken, but she heard it.

She slid off his lap, falling onto her knees. Begging for him to keep her, despite her silence.

"Stop that," he said, but his voice was more husky than angry now. "You're not my sub."

She wasn't his, but she had woken up in his home. Not his, but he had fucked her. And maybe more telling than all of that, he had fed her, taken her onto his lap, *helped* her. A man didn't do that for a woman who didn't belong to him.

But she wasn't so stupid as to say any of that aloud, even if she could have spoken. As usual he seemed to hear it anyway, his eyes flicking to her plate and back to her.

"Okay," he said. "I can see how you might have gotten that impression. But I'm not looking for a relationship, and especially not one…like this."

Her mind raced, looking for a way to convince him. Slowly, her gaze fell down over his broad shoulders, his red plaid shirt, his jeans. The bulge in his jeans. He said he didn't want her, but his body betrayed him, just like hers did.

She reached for him; he caught her wrists in a tight grip.

"What do you want, subby?" he asked, low and suggestive.

Looking up, she was caught by the intensity of his eyes. Black and electric. His stare alone seemed to touch her, reach inside and bring her to life.

Her breath came in small pants, and he looked down at her lips.

"You can't want this," he groaned, but he let her hands go. It was permission; in this position, it was an order. She undid his jeans and his cock, heavy and hard, fell into her palm. It throbbed once, and she floundered. Did he want her to touch him first? Or since he was already hard, should she put him in her mouth? She couldn't fail in this, not with him on the verge of sending her away. She looked up, for instruction, for approval.

The corner of his mouth turned up, the only smile she had seen from him. "Of course you would stop. You've been begging me, practically fucking me with those sexy blue eyes, but now you're going to think about it. Sometimes I think you get off on being contrary."

She shook her head, hard, to tell him no, she wanted to please him, but that only seemed to prove his words. He chuckled. The sound stirred something in her, something rusted with disuse.

"Then suck me, sweet girl. I know you know how."

She put her lips to his cock on the last word, a kiss to match the name he'd called her—sweet. Then she licked, and the salty tang of him burst onto her tongue. Finding the underside, she pleasured him, because he was right, she did know how. So well, too well.

This was different than all those other times, because she wanted this. And this was his cock, his pleasure. It didn't matter what he looked like, only that he seemed to want her and inexplicably she wanted him. What did she care about a man's anatomy? Well, if she had any preference it was for a smaller cock, because she'd be less likely to gag. He was big, but she wouldn't hold it against him.

Her breasts were pressed against the insides of his thighs as she fought to get closer, to take more of him, and she felt his muscles flex with every flick of her tongue. She laved the underside of his cock, and he jerked in her mouth. She swallowed him, and he groaned. She felt like she was sailing, fine-tuning the sails with her ministrations but ultimately at the mercy of the sea.

His thumb found her collarbone and swept back and forth, back and forth. "Christ, you're good at this. You know that, right?"

She paused and looked up at him, her mouth still full with his cock.

"Surely the men told you all about your hot mouth, your wicked tongue. Didn't they?"

He had to know she couldn't answer, but even the true question seemed unspoken. His eyes were dark with lust. And troubled, by something she couldn't comprehend.

He tangled his fingers in her hair and tightened. "You could own a man like that," he whispered.

His words surely weren't true; they were a puzzle. But maybe, yes. She swirled the tip with the right amount of suction that they always liked, and he let his head fall back. She found his balls, cupping them, rolling them, and he pumped his hips into the air. She wasn't stupid, for all that they'd called her that. She wasn't slow, though sometimes she felt that way. He was like any man; all he wanted was pleasure. That's what he must have meant. She could stay if she pleased him; yes, she knew.

When his hips jerked in a rhythm, it was time. She found a steady slide, in and out. The whore's technique; well, that was appropriate for her. Get him off, finish him a million times, so why did it feel different this time? Why did she feel so cold?

His semen was a warm splash at the back of her throat. She forced it down, trying to find appreciation in his shout. He'd lost control; they always did in that moment. She'd never figured out what to do with it, never really *wanted* to usurp them, but she knew men were brought low during climax.

As he fell back against the chair, his still-hard cock slipped from her mouth wetly, a trail of come stretching between them. She reached with her tongue to catch it, but it fell to the wood floor. Immediately she leaned in to lick it up, hopefully before he saw her and got too angry, but he stopped her.

"What are you doing?"

Her gaze drifted to the floor, that damnable wet spot that meant she hadn't followed the most basic of rules, she hadn't swallowed all of the come, she hadn't appreciated the gift.

"Leave it. I want you to leave it there." He definitely wasn't angry now, or even aroused. She recognized the look in his eyes now—sadness. "Touch yourself. I want to watch you make yourself come."

She shifted her weight where she knelt. This had been a small part of her training, near the beginning, when she could still have an orgasm. Sometimes it had worked; other times she had faked it. But the way his black gaze stripped her, she wouldn't be able to do that now. He was relaxed, prepared to wait, but all his attention was on her.

She pulled the dress up around her waist, exposing herself. But then she was already so bare, what was once more? Her fingers found her clit, rubbing tentatively at

34

the sensitive skin there. She felt a pinch of pain at the rough treatment but nothing like arousal. Nothing like pleasure.

She pressed harder, hurt herself faster under his intent gaze.

"Stop," he said.

He squatted in front of her and replaced her hand with his. His fingers swirled around her clit then skidded down along her sex. "Dry, dry as a fucking bone. And curled up tight. Are you afraid of me?"

She felt herself throb against his hand.

"Or maybe you're not afraid of me, and that's the problem. Is that what you need to get off? A little fear?" He slapped her lightly, the pain small but the sound loud. "A little pain?"

Her hips rocked against his hand, but what was this? Hadn't she dreamed, hoped for a day without fear—without pain? Now he'd offered her regular sex, painless sex, and she was too broken to do it.

His forehead came to rest on her shoulder, and her breath caught. It was a show of weakness, or it should have been, but he was so large, so intense, that it seemed to give support instead of take it. His palm cupped her below, just resting, feeling.

And then he began to speak. "I've got you. You're all turned around right now. Confused right now, but you're with me. I love these breasts; did you know that? So pale and sweet. Large too, for your body but I like them. They stand up proud. The only part of you that seems proud, sometimes. And your waist is too small, but it makes me hard anyway. I love to look at it,

35

especially from behind, the way it flares out into those hips."

Her body had relaxed, fallen loose in his embrace. His hand was still on her sex, and she was still dry, but she was relaxed. It was a start. She understood what he was doing. It was just another way to play with her, to manipulate her. Probably he didn't even mean the words, but it felt so good to believe.

He wanted her. He *saw* her. And if it were only her body that he saw, it would be enough. Maybe that's all there was left. But she didn't need to think of that, not when his hand had started a subtle roll against her skin, and he was still talking to her.

"I dreamed of you riding me at night. So dark, with only the faint light of moonlight on your breasts as they moved with you. It wouldn't be about what we could see though, but what we couldn't. You, panting above me. The sucking sounds of your cunt."

Somewhere around the word *sucking* it had happened: she'd begun to move her hips along with his hand. There was a rhythm there, a build. More, please, yes.

"I'd open my mouth and reach for your nipple, blindly because they're so dark. Rosy now, but black in the night. Your breasts would bounce against me, and I'd follow, turning my face, feeling with my tongue until I latched onto one and sucked."

There was the word again, different slightly but the same response. *Sucked.* She'd sucked a million times, hundreds of faceless cocks, and it hadn't meant a thing, but then he spoke the words. Soft, husky. Imbued with the promise of pleasure she felt now at her core. In her cunt. She tightened there, and his hand sped up, purposefully rubbing her clit. No pain now, no pinch, just relief.

"But here's what I really want to know. When I'm ready to come, I'll grab your hips and start thrusting up inside you. I won't be able to help it. And you'll grunt every time I do it, just a quick exhale. All automatic. And it'll hit a spot inside you so perfect that *you* won't be able to help it. You'll come around me. Gripping me, spilling your liquid all over my cock and down my balls."

She gripped him now, his fingers in her cunt. She spilled over him now, wet and needy. Faster, *almost*.

"But what I want to know is, will you cry out when you come? Would you speak for me then? What would you say?"

She came, she rocked, she lost her breath and found it again. She'd been given a gift, ungrateful. There was pleasure there and pain. Sweetness and betrayal. She bore witness to it all and mourned in silence.

"Shhh," he said. "Shhh." And she realized she was shaking. There were no words for it.

She'd never... she'd never...

"It's okay, little girl. I know you can talk."

She shook her head, her eyes shut tight, her head tucked into the crook of his neck. She'd never be normal again.

"I know you can talk because I heard you do it. When I found you, you spoke to me. You said you wanted to go home." He gave a rough laugh; it vibrated through her. "I tried to send you away, but damn you. I couldn't."

He crushed her to him tightly. "You're not going anywhere now."

CHAPTER FOUR

She followed the sound of destruction to the shed. Everything out here seemed rustic, though in truth it was sturdy and sleek to the touch, the shed almost as big as the house itself. She stood outside the door and stared at the sliver of light at the edges. She could return to the house, and he would never know she had strayed from his orders. But if she obeyed him, he would send her away. He'd already told her so.

Dust wafted in front of her face, making her sneeze. The buzzing sound stopped.

Master appeared at the door. He did not look pleased. "I told you to stay inside."

She looked down at her bare feet, coated with dust from the walk.

"Maybe you can come in. As long as you stay where I put you and don't ta—" He chuffed a small laugh, and something inside her relaxed fractionally. "Okay, girl. You can stay."

He opened the door wide to let her in. Orange glow suffused her vision, slowly sharpening into piles of furniture filling the room. There were tables, chairs, bookcases, and desks. As she looked closer, she could see that each piece had a small amount of engraving drawn into it. Somehow, the carvings didn't take over the piece— they looked as though they belonged there.

He pointed at a stool. "You can sit there."

She climbed onto the stool, running her fingers along the side, where vines were worked into the wood, complete with roses and thorns that pricked her. Beside her was a vanity with a carving at the base of the mirror.

There was a woman on a cliff, forlorn and haunting. Then out at sea, a ship caught in the storm with a single man at the helm. Penelope and Odysseus, she waited for her husband while he fought magic and nature to return home. Her throat felt tight. Her master's hands should terrify her, with their ability to hurt or restrain, but those hands had made this.

He returned to the worktable and began sanding a large contraption. At first she wasn't sure what it was. Her mind flew to some old style machinery for weaving, but that didn't make sense. She examined the lines across, the padding on the bottom rung—*oh*. It was meant to restrain a woman. She swallowed hard.

What would he do to a slave he bound there? There was so much she didn't know about him. Everything, really. She knew he ate sparingly for his size, he lived simply. She knew his hands were coarse but precise when they carved into wood, when they held her body down.

She knew he wanted her.

He said he didn't. It had almost seemed as if he hadn't known she was a slave. As if he hadn't purchased her and brought her to his home. He promised to send her away every time he spoke, but still he hadn't. Even though she had asked to go home, he had kept her.

Possession. Servitude. This was what she had trained for, and he was a kinder Master than she would have thought possible.

His eyebrows drew together as he worked. His movements grew slower, more careful. The hard planes of his face had softened in the glow of the lamp, a lock of black hair fell over his eyes. He raised a different sort of awareness in her than obedience, as well, one of a woman to a man.

The way he focused on it was the way he focused on her, and she longed to see the outpouring of his intensity. In the same way she would trace any marks he granted her body, she wanted to see the wounds he cut into the wood.

He straightened and stretched his arms. His eyes caught hers.

"Bored, are you?" He swung his arms down, tilted his head from side to side as if to loosen tight muscles. "Told you to stay in the house. There's books at least, if you like reading about metalworking."

It almost sounded like teasing, the way his voice lowered. She cocked her head to the side.

"Come here." He stepped aside to make room. At her hesitation, he said, "Don't worry. I'm not planning on using this."

She carefully stepped down from the bench and approached him. Truly, she knew better than this. A master was capricious, unstable. Harsh on the best days, but oh, there was worse. But his quiet intensity was a balm to unseen wounds. His stark kindness more seductive than the painful vibrating wands they used to induce her orgasms.

Looking down at the contraption, she tried to ignore his size, his heat at her side. At first it seemed that this piece had no carvings, until she cautiously circled the bench and saw the markings on the bottom rung. And they were upside down. She tilted her head, so that she could see the scene the same way a woman who was tied down on the bench would see it.

Another scene from *The Odyssey*. This time a woman with long golden hair stood naked on the beach while Odysseus was tied to the mast of his ship, desperate and wanting.

"Do you like it?" There was an uncertainty in his gruff voice that said this mattered.

It wasn't simply the artwork that was beautiful, it was the reverence to the person who would be imprisoned here, hurt here. *I'm just as much a slave as you*, this said. She nodded.

He studied her. "I think you do understand. It's your eyes. You speak with them."

She stared up into his remote brown ones and wished he did that too. Looking up at him, the way his thick lashes framed his eyes, something stirred in her mind. Something dark and sinister, and she pushed it back where it couldn't frighten her.

He turned back to the bench. "I'm making this for my brother, for his wedding present. He'd rather have this than a cheese platter. He runs an import/export business, and he already ships most of my stuff between here and the mainland. So there's no reason I shouldn't send it."

He looked at her as if she might object then sighed when she didn't. "I should be over it by now. Maybe that's why you ended up here, subby. To teach me about forgiveness, about letting go of all this damned ugly pride. Well, tell me. What's the secret then?"

Her gaze fell to the floor, demurring.

"No." He lifted her chin. "There's been enough looking at the floor. Look at me."

She tried, but everything was a blur. He wiped a tear from her cheek.

"None of that either. At least, not unless I'm trying to hurt you. Here, give me a few minutes to clean up here and then I want to show you something. You've been a good girl. You deserve a reward."

She jumped when she saw an iguana, only relaxing when she saw it was as still as the rock it sat on. He shook his head, but she could tell from the curve of his lips that he wasn't really angry. His whole demeanor had relaxed since she had intruded on his work, and in her relief that she wasn't in trouble, she relaxed too. The way they walked together was different too. She wasn't following him, but walked beside. Wasn't cowed by him, instead adoring. It felt wrong and delicious at the same time. If she suffered later, this would be worth it.

They walked along a well-worn path that eventually turned into rocks. When she winced at a sharp one under her bare foot, he paused. "Damn, I didn't think of that. Do we need to go back?"

She was out of breath, exhilarated. *No. Please.*

He grinned, at least that's what the small curve of his lips seemed like. Even that much seemed blinding. "What are we going to do then?" He didn't wait for an answer, just pulled off his own boots and socks.

"Come on." He grabbed her hand and they ran across the beach, throwing up white rocks in their wake. She felt herself smiling, and when he looked at her, she could have sworn she saw awe in his eyes.

They entered a cave of some sort, with a pool of water below and rock surrounding them on three sides. Emerald light streamed inside through an opening in the top and, filtered through the thick mist in the air, cast colors all around. She lifted a hand to touch the green-purple and caught only air. Below, the water sparkled, a melting pot of color, all above a deep black void.

It took her breath away.

"Like it?" he asked, sounding just like he had in his workshop.

What do you want, girl?

She kissed him. His lips were unexpectedly soft. They parted—in surprise, she thought—and then she slipped her tongue inside. It had been forever since she'd done this, never had she done this, but it came to her like breathing. She needed it, and if he took it away, if he stopped her...

43

He did stop her, but only to reverse everything, changing it but leaving it the same, with only the flick of his tongue and the tightening of his hand on her hip. Then it was him kissing her; it was her sighing. *Please, oh please.* And he answered her with his heat, his taste, with the pleasure he found from showing her this place of beauty and magic.

No, she'd been wrong. Any price would be too high if she were to lose this after all. Even precious courtesy wouldn't be enough, compared to this. The world upended around her, from pain to pleasure, from survival to passion. The pebbled beach smoothed to velvet under her feet, the moisture in the air slicked their skin.

An ache started in her sex, and her hips rocked against him. She would have restrained herself once she noticed, but he moaned, and she knew without words that it was good. She was good, and he wanted her to keep doing it. So she let her body lead—strange though it felt, foreign and uncertain. She rolled her body along his, she ran her hands over his skin.

It wasn't her anyway. This was too much, too fast. It had to be some other woman playing the sensual lover, because she would never dare. And when he said, "God, yes, so long," it was only a dream.

He broke the kiss, and she sighed with regret. But then he pulled her to the water, where eddies of warm and cool tickled her feet. She gasped in delight, and it sounded sharply even over the rush inside the cave. It had a strange amplifying effect—even the silence was loud, but each small splash or sigh was a roar in her ears.

She looked up to find him watching her with an enigmatic expression. In the shadows, the darkness of his eyes loomed large. She imagined she could see his thoughts, that they swirled like so much smoke: thick bands of lust, wisps of amusement.

Her training wasn't about how to stand or to suck, not really. She had become an expert at reading expressions, at decoding body language. He was a formidable cipher, but she only needed time.

Meanwhile, she knew well enough what those heavy lids and flattened lips meant. She saw the tinge of red on his cheeks. All of that would have told her, even if she hadn't seen the bulge in his wet jeans. He wanted to take her and this time, it wasn't in his sleep. It wasn't in some awkward moment, born of pity—no. He had initiated this. He had brought her to this magical place. No dream.

He seemed to like her forwardness, like a release valve to the curious guilt he had about her status, so she tentatively reached up to sweep a wet lock of hair from his forehead. He remained still for her touch, his expression one of approving forbearance. But when she went to stroke down his neck, he caught her wrist.

"I'm going to ask you something, and I want you to say no if you don't want it too. I'm afraid you can't. If I were better—stronger—I wouldn't even make you choose, but I…" He sighed. The moisture in the air beaded on his eyelashes. "It's been so long. I've waited so long."

He pulled her in deeper, until the water climbed her thighs and lapped at her cunt. They followed the wall of the cave until it opened up onto a small beach that was completely enclosed by cool stone and reflective water. Barely enough place for both of them, but she knew that was the point. Here even the white noise of the water was reduced, and all she could hear was her breath and his.

"I never imagined a submissive as perfect as you," he said lowly, but the words were as commanding as she'd ever heard him. "I keep thinking you're not real, that I'll wake up and find myself alone again. But this isn't real, is it? You aren't really like this. They made you this way."

Don't make me think about it. Just want me.

"Jesus Christ," he said. "When you look at me, so damn trusting. It's not right. I know that, but I can't stop. Will you let me, subby? Can I hurt you?"

Her only hesitation was how best to answer him—*yes,*

anything, finally—and she slowly left the water, let it fall off her body as she sank to her knees. To her surprise, there weren't any sharp pebbles here—only silky sand beneath her palms, sliding up between her fingers. Not part of the rough ground outside, this was an extension of the ocean floor, worn smooth from an eternity of ripples.

She glanced back to gauge her behavior; he stared at her body with such blatant appreciation that she felt a flush of pride mingle with the slow burn of arousal.

"You have to promise to stop me." He gave her a light smack on the flat of her ass. "Can you snap your fingers? Let me see you do it."

She did, and he hit her again. It was light, more of a promise than a punishment. It bore little resemblance to the spankings she had endured at the hands of other men. She had been cold and shaken, like a cymbal played too loud and too long. But now his hands moved over her skin like a melody long forgotten.

Then she forgot to listen to the slap of his hand on her skin, the gentle backdrop of trickling water fell away. There was only feeling; there was only pleasure. And all of it underscored with the rhythm of her body into his.

She almost didn't notice when he stopped, because the beat continued in her body. It narrowed in her clit as he touched her there. Her fingers were clenched in the sand, she realized. Her body rocked over his hand, using it for its sweet pressure. This was wanton, it was release.

Despite her nakedness, despite his fingers in her cunt and his hoarse words urging her on, this was the least sexual thing she had ever done. It wasn't even submission, at least not as she had known it. It was freedom.

She couldn't think if she was pleasing him. She couldn't think if he might hurt her. She couldn't think, not at all. Pleasure sang through her body, spiraled higher and shuddered through her. Her climax came upon her from behind, where he was, murmuring words against her shoulder. *Yes, like that, so beautiful.*

Aftershocks racked her body, and he held her through all of it. The long weight of his body, his thick arms, were like a cage around her, and yet she felt safe. The hard length of his cock pressed against her ass, and that at least was something familiar. Something she could recognize from the old, but even that didn't scare her. It would hurt, it always did, and so what?

He waited for her to recover. She knew that from that way he held himself so tightly leashed. Though she was still weak, still tender, she pushed back against him. It didn't feel strange, giving him permission. Her body gave it for her. But he caught her hip in a tight grip. His fingers dug into her soft flesh.

"Wait," he ground out. "Damn—I can't. Just don't move."

After a minute he pushed back, letting the moist air mingle with the sweat on her back and her fluid on her thighs. She turned back, expecting to see him unzipping, maybe directing her to her knees, but he had turned away. He was already wading into the water by the time she stood up. He moved too fast through the water, and she couldn't keep up.

On the other side of the water, he emerged and kept going. It was on the pointy rocks where she finally caught his arm.

He turned back, and she shrank away from the fire burning in them. "Fuck, don't look at me like that. Don't look at me at all. Don't you know what your eyes do to me? And where the fuck are your clothes? No. No, don't go back and get them."

He gently held her arms and rested his forehead against hers. The rocks dug into her soles, and that was why her eyes were wet, that was why.

"Damn you, I'm trying to be honorable here." His breath caught on a laugh that hurt her to hear. "I know I'm failing. That's why I wanted you to go, but I can't give you up either. So what are we going to do? Can you tell me

47

that, subby?"

She didn't have an answer for him. He swung her up into his arms and carried her like the proverbial bride across the threshold, if the bride were a slave of questionable consent and the threshold tore his feet.

Tucking her head against his shoulder, she watched him leave flecks of red on the chalk-white pebbles. He left his own blood behind just to spare hers. He had lied. He'd said he was going to hurt her, but he was the one who was hurt. Her body clenched in a phantom pain, and he followed her glance to see the trail of blood.

His look was wry. "At least it's distracting me from the other problem."

She stroked his jaw, where stubble had thickened.

He pressed a quick kiss against her lips. The fullness of his lips against hers was always a surprise, considering how hard they always seemed when he looked at her. "Forget what I said before. Don't worry."

It was impossible to obey that order, but at least she could pretend. She could narrow her focus to the practical, so that when he finally relinquished her at the door of his cottage, she ran inside in search of bandages and creams.

At least he let her tend his feet. Kneeling in front of him, she eyed the undiminished rise in his jeans.

He shook his head firmly. "No, subby. Not yet."

When? she thought, but thank goodness she couldn't speak.

CHAPTER FIVE

She hated waking because of the uncertainty. The fear that this had only been a momentary delusion, the child of a painful subspace coma. She took a moment to convince herself this was real, rubbing the cotton sheets, counting the planks in the ceiling. She would have touched her Master too, but she couldn't risk waking him. Besides, his gentle snores were real enough. She almost smiled. It wasn't likely her dreams would have conjured that.

The moonlight shone brightly through the window, illuminating his coarse features. It occurred to her that she could trick him into having intercourse with her. Likely he was already hard. If she touched him now, he might fuck her in his sleep like before. She didn't feel guilt over what had happened then, it had been purely accidental, completely unexpected.

But if she made any overtures now, it would be willful. A deliberate attempt to make him have sex with her when he had already said no. She couldn't do that to him. She couldn't be like the men who had hurt her.

No matter how she tried to rationalize it in her head, the part of her that knew right from wrong stubbornly refused to die. Even though it might increase their intimacy and thus better secure her place here, she couldn't defile him that way.

A few sips of water might settle her nerves. She would have lapped at her bowl if she were still imprisoned, but now she could get up and retrieve a glass of water herself. It had been startlingly easy to fall into this new role, one where she made requests, not pleas. One where she did for herself instead of waiting. It made her consider just how long her slavery had really been.

It made her wonder what came before.

Pushing that unwelcome thought aside, she found her way through the hallway. Without the light of the large window, the rest of the house was nothing but shadows. She filled a glass; the splash of water was loud, reminding her of the rushing waterfall from earlier today. The faucet turned off with a squeak.

She paused, staring at the dark ripples in the cup she held. By slow degrees she became aware of an echo of her own breath. The hair on her neck raised. She wasn't alone in the room.

"What are you doing out of bed?" came the low voice from the corner.

Master!

How had he managed to slip past her without her noticing? It didn't matter. He was there. His voice sounded different, like the low voice he had used to tease her, but more. As if he knew a big joke that she didn't. She felt an answering smile on her own face, but it was slanted with her confusion. And her worry. He was kind when stoic, he had spanked her when playful, what did this new side of him mean?

He was closer now. "A pretty little slave knows better than to wander away."

Then she recognized that tone: cruelty. Just this morning she had marveled at his lack of it. Now it appeared she would see its face, even if it was still too dark to see his.

She had the urge to flee, but where would she go? She had the urge to fall down at his feet, but he had always hated it when she did that.

"How quickly you forget yourself," he said in a musing tone.

A gasp escaped her, but it was too late. He caught her by the arm and yanked her to him. Off balance, she would have tumbled into his body, but he turned to the side. She landed face-first on the floor with him following close behind, on top of her.

She panted, thoroughly subdued before she had even thought to fight.

"No one will hear you if you scream. But then, you can't scream, can you?" He spoke low against her shoulder just like earlier, but this was different. The rumbling of his voice dragged through her body like barbs down her back. There was none of the pleasure.

None of the care. She had not realized how gentle he had been with her before. She had been far too distracted by the feelings coursing through her cunt, her breasts. But now all she felt was his hand on her neck, pressing her face into the lumpy wood floor. And the feel of his cock lying against her ass made her squirm.

He grunted. "Maybe we had the wrong idea all along. Maybe I don't need your obedience. I like it when you struggle."

Perhaps it was a spark of panic at this new sadistic side of him or perhaps it was a perverse desire to please him, but she renewed her struggles. She attempted to push up, but his grip on her neck was like iron. She reached back, hitting nothing, kicking no one. As her body writhed against his, he groaned. After she had flailed and managed to bruise her own body against the wooden floor, she sank down in defeat.

"Is that all you've got?" he taunted in a whisper. "I like that. Just a little bit of spirit so I don't feel like I'm fucking a piece of meat. But then you'll settle down and take it, won't you?"

A shiver ran through her, and he laughed softly. He kicked her knees out, spreading them wide. Her fingers scrabbled against the wood, finding nothing to hold on to. There'd be no pleasure here. No passion, no solace.

His cock nudged her entrance, blunt and hard, but at least the first drops of his orgasm provided much needed lubrication. In one smooth, angry motion, he slid to the hilt. She gasped.

"Talk, dammit," he muttered behind her. "What the fuck is wrong with you? Even if you can't say the words, you ought to be able to make noise."

He pulled out and slammed back in. Her entire body seemed to ripple upon impact, rattling apart and then slamming back together. But still, she was silent but for her harsh breathing.

"How hard would I have to hurt you," he whispered in her ear, "before you screamed?"

She felt her eyes widen, but then they slammed shut again as he thrust deep inside. Her body felt broken in pieces, disjointed. Her mind was lost, confused, hurt more by Master's sudden shift in temperament than she had been for the weeks, months before.

It was one thing to be treated like an animal night and day; she could almost believe it was true. Her mindlessness became a refuge; her submission a balm. But he had treated her like so much more: a desired lover, a cherished slave.

Somehow she had ruined it.

Her fragile happiness lay on the floor of the kitchen in shards, plowed again and again by the fierce iron cock of her Master. It shouldn't have been able to hurt anymore; it cut her open. Her eyes stung, and throat felt raw. It was a cry for help, empty, soundless.

He groaned, a long exhalation that shook the air around her, moving it when she could not. Filling it with his satisfaction where her pain should have gone. The heat and weight of his body fell onto hers, flattening her. She was so far wrung out that there should be nothing left, as she struggled to draw breath under the pressure.

But a part of her burned, doused by the wind only to flare up on its reprieve. She no longer thought of survival alone; she wanted more. This afternoon he'd been lenient with her. Generous with her. And in doing so, he'd damned them both.

The air cooled behind her; it stilled. She was alone but found no relief.

She could leave. If she walked outside now, her chances would be better than they had been on her first escape. Better, because now she was full and warm to begin with. Maybe she could even pack supplies, find money to help her. These practical thoughts fell one after the other, a line of lanterns on a string. Somewhere inside her was a self-sufficient woman, trapped by her training. Silenced by terror.

Her head cocked to the side. She heard nothing. He must have gone back to bed.

She stood up, intending to leave. Surely she would at least make the attempt, even though a larger part of her doubted her ability to succeed. More than that she doubted her sanity, but then, didn't every animal wish to be free? Or perhaps she was so contented as his pet despite his recent rough treatment that she wished to stay.

The desire for freedom felt familiar, like an old friend. It brought a burst of happiness, just the glimpse of it, but she wasn't sure she really knew it after all this time. Had she ever really?

She found herself walking into the living room. Just to search for supplies, she reasoned. Here the moonlight was a bit brighter than the kitchen, and she could just make out the striped corduroy of the sofa and the low thick coffee table she now recognized as having been made by her master's hand.

The bookcase was overstuffed, with small books

jammed sideways, toppling over one another in an attempt to fit in. Each book wore its use like a badge of honor, the spine cracked and stripped from being bent open. A corollary to the scars on her back; she shivered.

The only other piece of furniture in the room was a black trunk in the corner. Unlike the books, it was gray with dust and disuse. She wondered that it was not wood. It would have stuck out with its leather siding and garish gold corners, if it had not been so clearly shoved away. Unwanted.

She fiddled with the lock, expecting resistance, but the top opened with only the slightest creak. The top layer was black fabric, probably meant to protect what was underneath. At one time, someone had cared about these contents. She was like an archaeologist, peeling back the layers to determine what once was.

Her fingers touched on leather, and she lifted out a flogger. It was large and heavy, though not intimidating to her. She knew it would make a pleasant thud on her flesh, not sting or mark. Though how she knew that was a mystery, since nothing she had experienced in captivity had been pleasant, and she most definitely had never been allowed to hold an implement.

Tucking that thought away, she reached in again. There were padded leather cuffs, yards and yards of rope. Everything a kinky person might desire; all of it intended to hurt but not harm. There was safety built in, *care* built in to every item. It was shocking to her, and then, not surprising at all.

She'd always known it wasn't right. But there were only so many times her mind could scream for justice, for mercy, before it turned on her. Twisted her own beliefs until she thought up was down, bad was good, and slavery was life.

There were dildos and nipple clamps, some more scary than others but none of it vicious. She unraveled a soft leather package to find a sleek knife. She shivered. Knife play? Maybe she had been too quick to judge no harm, but she didn't think so. They were too clean and their wrapping too meticulous. This wasn't something taken lightly. Safety. Care.

She wouldn't have minded these, but she knew they weren't meant for her. She was the interloper here, touching cold metal and glass that had once been warmed by a body... but whose?

She found the answer at the bottom. By now she sat amid a sea of sex toys. The thought flitted through her head: what if he found her this way? But it passed quickly, eclipsed by her curiosity and perplexing but growing certainty that her true freedom lay somewhere in here.

The collar was thin black leather, very soft and supple. It had a ring in the front of it and an inscription along the inside.

Master's Lovely Pet

Her heart contracted for this woman she never knew, for love lost. She knew with sudden certainty that the woman was dead. She knew she'd been loved.

One by one, she replaced every item in the trunk. The collar, the knives, the little clover nipple clamps in their clear plastic box. She laid the black blanket over the top and shut the lid, throwing up a cloud of dust that tickled her nose. Her idea to run had been put away as well for the silliness it was.

She had no memory of where she came from, no future outside these walls. There was only a man, gruff and tender, haunted but hopeful. A thought came to her that she could aspire to this, a beloved pet, but she let it slip from her grasp. It didn't matter. To be with him enough and everything all at once.

She climbed into bed, beside the softly snoring form of her Master. The euphoria of the day had been stripped from her, but there was still a quiet satisfaction in servitude. Always that. Only that.

It was the smell of bacon she noticed first, making her mouth water before she'd fully come awake. But it was the sound of male voices in conversation that drew her upright, and quickly.

Had they found her?

Although if they had really come to take her away, surely they wouldn't have let her sleep in. The bed was still musky with her master's scent, her own body still aching from his anger. He wouldn't let them take her, she hoped. But oh, he had seemed so different last night.

Another dress lay on the bed, this time a white sheath with bright red flowers. It was such the opposite of fetish-wear or sexy lingerie. She crushed it between her fingers before slipping it over her head.

She gave brief thought to remaining in his room until she'd been called, but for all she knew the clothes had been tacit instruction for her to come out. This master seemed to want her to show initiative. He didn't punish her when she got it wrong either; he just corrected her. And what's more, she liked showing initiative.

She also found that, with him, she liked being corrected.

Her curiosity won out, and she slipped down the hall and stood outside the kitchen.

"That's all in the past," said a voice she recognized as her master's. "We don't have to go over it again. There's nothing more to be said."

"I'd agree if you weren't still fucking pouting about it," said another voice. It was slightly higher than her master's, but only just. It was more the way he spoke that set him apart.

"I'm not pouting, I just don't need it dredged up every time you don't like what I'm doing."

"What do you call hiding away in the middle of fucking nowhere, Sam? And I'm not complaining about the color curtains you've put up. There's a person at stake here. She needs help, not a spanking."

"Fuck you, Brendan. It's none of your business."

"She's a mess. She's broken. Do you think you're helping things by fucking her? Have you got a magic prick, is that it?"

The table slammed. "Don't talk about her that way."

There was silence.

"Okay, brother. Okay. Take it easy. I'm worried about you too. You don't even know her. What if she's taking you for a ride?"

"Are you worried she's trying to swindle me out of my dining tables?" her master asked dryly.

"You and I both know you're more than a goddamned carpenter."

"You're right," her master said. "I should visit the beach today. Maybe I can walk on water after all."

"Very funny. What about what she wants? Do you think she wants to be stuck out in the middle of nowhere?"

She held her breath to hear her master's answer.

Finally he spoke slowly, "Why don't you ask her yourself? She's standing outside the door. Come in here." The last was for her.

She stepped out in the doorway, keeping her eyes downcast. Though this time her lowered gaze wasn't only a symbol of submission but of fear. She didn't want to know, didn't want to confirm the suspicion that had gnawed at her since she'd first heard the voice of her master's brother. Last night... in the dark, he had sounded different. She had thought it was a result of whispering in the night, a result of whatever mood had made him cruel. But if he'd simply been a different person...

"Well, subby?" her master asked, not unkindly. "Do you want to leave here? He's got a boat tied up just down the beach. You can be on your way to the mainland in a few minutes."

She shook her head no, vehemently. Daring a glance,

she saw her master's eyes glitter with triumph.

"You heard her," he said. "She wants to stay."

"I didn't hear her at all," his brother said wryly. "She hasn't said a word to you?"

She remembered: *When I found you, you spoke to me. You said you wanted to go home.*

"We get along just fine," her master said. "I figure that's part of being a good Dom—reading the body language of your sub."

"Right. And you were always the good Dom, weren't you?" He stood. "I have business to take care of, but I'm not leaving the islands until tonight. You have until then to come to your senses."

He made to leave but stopped beside her. She could see how she'd mistaken him in the dark. He looked just like his brother: the same height and muscled build. The same strong features, with shadows cut into his cheeks and stubble dotting his jaw.

The difference was that while her master seemed to wear jeans and a plain white T-shirt, and maybe the occasional plaid shirt, his brother wore sleek beige slacks and a sharp polo. While her master had dark hair and darker eyes, Brendan was blond with brown eyes that looked unnaturally light, as if she could see through them. His face had more laugh lines than her master's, but somehow she wasn't comforted by his humor.

His lingering gaze made her skin crawl, even beneath the lovely modest dress. Leaning back, he stared at her knees, and in his eyes she saw knowledge that damned them both. "Are those bruises I see? I hope my brother hasn't been too rough with you."

After he left the room, her master lifted the hem of her dress to examine her knees. "They are a little black and blue. When did that happen—on the beach?" He looked up into her eyes.

It doesn't hurt, she tried to convey. Although she did feel sick to her stomach now.

"I suppose I can't tell you that you should've said something. But you should have. That's what the safeword was for. You were supposed to snap if it was too much."

She gestured to the floor behind her but then let her hand fall at her side. There'd be no way to communicate that she'd actually gotten the bruises on the floor. And even if she could say so, she wouldn't. He could never know what she had done.

Even though she hadn't had a choice, hadn't even known it was betrayal at the time, he could never know that his brother had fucked her. She felt sure of it, from the competitive way they treated each other to the possessive way her master looked at her. He wouldn't have shared her willingly, and he wouldn't be happy to know it had happened while he slept.

If she wanted to stay here—and oh, she did—then she would have to keep it a secret. Well that wouldn't be too hard for her, after all. It was his brother Brendan she was worried about.

"I suppose you wouldn't say it was too much, would you? Wouldn't think so after what you've been through. Those marks on your body..." He looked at the door where his brother had left. "I'm going out for a walk today. I was planning on taking you, but now I don't know."

If he left her here she would be at Brendan's mercy, and surely he would hurt her again, fuck her again. She shook her head, pleading with her eyes.

"I can't trust you to tell me when something is wrong out there. You're safer here."

I'm not, she thought fiercely. *I'm not safe here with your brother.*

He frowned. "Maybe he's right about you. About us. I didn't want to send you off alone with strangers in a uniform. I figured they could do more harm than good, not understanding what you needed. But Brendan's a Dom too. He can take care of you."

No. Please no. Brendan scared her but more than that,

she was healing under her master's hand. Already she felt more able to think for herself, and she was terrified to lose it again.

His expression softened. "It won't be so bad. He always knows the right thing to say." He gave her an echo of a smile. "Most people prefer him to me anyway."

Strangely it was his softening that alarmed her the most, as if he were apologizing for a decision already made.

"Please." It was a breath of a sound, and it came from her.

His eyes widened a fraction as her word floated on the air between them. Slowly he leaned back in his chair, like a contented cat. "So, subby, you really do want to stay."

CHAPTER SIX

Apparently going for a walk included chopping down trees. He was a veritable lumberjack, her master. She found it adorable, although she doubted he would appreciate her sentiment. He wouldn't know, of course. She hadn't spoken since that one word in the kitchen.

He hadn't tried to push her to talk more. He hadn't even made a big deal out of the fact that she had, just went about his preparations for their walk, asking a couple of yes or no questions to which she nodded or shook her head. A weight had lifted. She knew she *could* speak. She just didn't have to.

Ironically, her speaking seemed to have spurred on his own. He had sat her on a rock uphill so that he could measure and *touch* the trees.

"I don't do this too often," he panted, between swinging his ax. "Mostly I have the wood imported. I know that sounds strange, what with all these trees around, but I don't want to do damage while I'm here. I just take a couple trees for smaller projects. This wood works beautifully for smaller carvings."

Every thwack of wood resounded around her, through her, creating a strange emphasis to his words. As if there were something important in them—vital.

"The wood I order comes from sustainable farms on the mainland and considering my brother came this way anyway, it wasn't much trouble for him to include my wood on the way in and my furniture on the way out."

The tree fell over, swishing through the air and landing with a crash.

"Although now that his business here is over, I guess I'll need a new plan."

Suddenly she knew what she needed to ask. "What did he import?"

It was surprising how effortless it was to speak. Her voice sounded low but not hoarse.

He paused then strode quickly up to where she sat. "What did you say?"

She thrilled to see the banked excitement in his eyes, to know that he cared about her and what she had to say, but something heavier weighed on her now. "His shipping business. What does he ship?"

Master cocked his head. "Parts for manufacturing, for building. Once he got to transport a shipload of Maseratis. I think that was the high point. It's mostly boring stuff. Why do you ask?"

"Just curious…Master."

His look seared her. "You can call me by name." He stepped directly in front of her and held out his hand. "I'm Sam. Nice to meet you."

She stared at it curiously, large and calloused and inexplicably familiar. Finally she reached out, and he took her hand and pulled her to him. She was enfolded in his arms, tucked under his chin, and she never wanted to leave.

"What's your name?" he asked.

"…don't know."

"Okay," he said, accepting her words as if it were completely normal not to know her own name. As if *she* were normal.

"Number forty-five," she mumbled. "Slave forty-five."

She curled into his embrace, as if she could climb inside him, breathe only his musk, and be the beat of his heart. He smoothed her hair, ran his hands along her arms, still answering her unspoken pleas even though she could speak.

"I know this must be scary for you," he murmured. "I'm going to help you however I can, but one day you'll go back. No, shhh, not right now. You don't have to leave tonight. But we could try to contact someone. Surely there are people who miss you, who want to know that you're okay. A family." He paused a beat. "A husband. Can you remember any of it?"

"Can't... she doesn't... she doesn't know."

The silence was stark then, so complete between them that the faint buzz of a nearby insect intruded. Nothing had fazed him, not the scars on her body, her overly submissive ways, or even her inability to speak. But now he seemed at a loss, *she* was at a loss, unable to even say the word *I*.

I don't know, was what she had meant to say, but even in her mind she tripped over it. Like she wasn't even a person anymore. How much had they taken from her? Too much, now this.

"Subby." His voice raw, as if he'd been shouting. "Who did this to you?"

She swallowed. "I...I..."

I think it was your brother.

Her memories from her old prison were muted but clear enough to make out faces. She had never seen him there, even though her skin tingled with sick familiarity when he touched her last night. But even if he hadn't abused her, she suspected he was involved with them. How much shipping industry could there be in a group of islands?

More than that, he had known. He had known that she couldn't speak, he'd known that she had been trained. All without ever meeting her before.

But she only had to get through today. He would be gone tonight.

"How often does he come? Your…your…Brendan?"

"Maybe every few weeks. Sometimes a couple of months go by. Why?"

"Rather be alone." *With you.*

He squeezed my arm. "I suppose you're attached to me because I was the one to find you. But you don't have to worry about my brother. Not all men are like the ones who hurt you."

She looked down, wishing she could believe it.

"He's a good guy." His gaze was off into the trees, far away. "We didn't used to get along. When we were kids, we were competitive. Even when we grew up, we would keep in touch just trying to one-up the other. Then something… something happened. I want to say it's all his fault. For a long time I did think so, but I take responsibility for it now."

He paused, and she thought he wouldn't continue. She nuzzled her nose into his chest to prompt him. His gaze snapped back to the present, to her, and he smiled slightly. Then it faded.

"We used to Dom together. It was just something we did. There isn't any excuse for it. It wasn't that we just shared the girls… we used them. Pushing them harder and farther and longer just because we had something to prove."

He sighed. "Then I met a woman. We started dating, then she moved in. Pretty soon she was subbing twenty-four seven, like you. I had so much damn pride. Too much. Then I found out she was seeing my brother."

A small sound escaped her. She had some idea of where this was going now, of the part she had played in this sibling rivalry. It had been bad enough knowing she had betrayed a nameless Master, distant and aloof from herself, but now that he was opening up to her, now that she knew how much harder he would take it...

"We had shared her when we started dating, only once, and I knew that would be the last time. When I found out she was still seeing him, I went a little crazy. I broke up with her. Didn't even pay attention to the fact that she was totally dependent on me, just kicked her out. She got mugged and killed a few days later."

He looked down at her, eyes like swirling mercury. "I finally gave up the fight. Moved down here. So my brother won after all. At least that's what I thought. But her death affected him too. He came down to visit me, saw some of my furniture, and carted it back to the states. This is as close as we've ever been."

A sudden premonition that she would ruin this fragile peace left her cold. Surely she wasn't important enough to warrant that. She was a piece of trash he found on the beach, not a treasured lover. Not his lovely pet. She shivered.

"We should head back." Abruptly, he stood, catching me from falling off his lap with a firm grip. "Hey. Don't worry. Everything will be just fine. You can talk to him at dinner tonight. Who knows? You two might hit it off."

The savory smell of the steaks that Brendan had brought simmered in the air. Her mouth watered even as her stomach turned over. She was a bundle of nerves, a mass of fear. If Sam found out that Brendan had fucked her, he wouldn't only cast her off, he would give her to Brendan.

Maybe worse than that, she had to get through a meal with Brendan. It wasn't just what he had done to her. She had been hurt before, worse. He didn't seem especially cruel. There was something about him that made her skin crawl with both wariness and recognition.

She slipped on the dress Sam had laid out for her, a soft purple one that flared out at her hips and ended mid-thigh. She had figured out by now that these clothes had belonged to the woman Sam had loved.

It was only a little bit creepy to wear the clothes of a dead woman. After all, the cell she inhabited had been covered in a gooey metallic substance when she arrived, and it hadn't taken a genius to figure out what had happened. Any squeamishness she might have had in a former life was long gone.

It was more that wearing the woman's clothes served to underline that she didn't wear the collar too. It underlined her complete and utter lack of permanence here. He did seem to want her and had about admitted as much, which was an improvement over when she had first arrived. But that was a long cry from wanting to keep her... preferably forever. Ironically, he seemed to think she would want to leave soon, but she wouldn't.

As she stepped out of the cabin, he turned to face her and raised his eyebrows. "You look good, subby. How are you with a knife?"

He set her up with a pile of onions and a chopping block. "Slice them thick for the grill," he said.

She went to work, but paused to push a strand of hair back from her face with her forearm. He hadn't included any sort of tie for her hair. The muscles of his forearm caught her eye. Her gaze traveled upward to where a lock of black hair curled over his brow. No, she didn't want to leave, it wasn't anything to do with how handsome he was, in his own dark way. It wasn't because he made her feel safe. Not even because he had woken her from the prison of her own mind.

It was because he made her think of the future. She could see them together: watching him work with the wood, cooking together under the warm sunset, having kinky sex in the sweetly sticky nights. It was a fantasy, a fairy tale, but it was *more*. She had slipped out of survival mode without even realizing it. Her thoughts weren't consumed with avoiding the next blow or earning the next meal. Thinking back on how she'd been only a few days ago, terrified and broken—it was like waking from a nightmare, sweaty, heart-pounding.

His hand on hers startled her. "Be careful there. Can you even see anymore?"

She couldn't, not with the tears in her eyes. The knife slipped from her fingers, and she let him take it. *Trust*, that's what it was. Even with all of their power, as cowed as she was, the men at the compound would never have handed her a knife. Even then, she would have used it on them.

Sam trusted her.

"Hey. What's this?" He pulled her in for a hug. She breathed him in, once again enclosed in him, safe with him on a hill in the woods. "You don't have to tell me if you don't want to. Whatever it is, I'll keep you safe."

"Very sweet," came Brendan's voice, and something stirred within her, like remembrance. "Am I intruding?"

Sam had tensed when Brendan came out; he relaxed by degrees. Though he said that his brother was harmless, there was some instinct that remained wary. "Of course not," Sam said. "The food's almost ready. Why don't you set the table?"

"Sure thing, brother," Brendan said with an enigmatic smile that sent a shiver down her spine.

Even when Brendan returned inside to the table, Sam and she worked in silence, the air shimmering with tension. She carried in a plate of steaks while Sam finished grilling the vegetables.

Brendan stood when she came in and took the plate from her. "Here," he said. "Have a seat next to me."

She eyed the chair on the far end with longing.

"That's no good," Brendan chided. "You're a sight for sore eyes. The prettiest thing I've seen in weeks. Months even. You wouldn't deny me the pleasure, would you?"

Her trepidation rose at his flowery words, meant to trick and subvert.

"Ah, brother," Brendan said. "You finally made it. Tell your girl here to have a seat before she falls over."

Sam frowned, but he said slowly, "Sit down, subby."

She did.

"Good." Brendan sat beside her. "Right in the middle. We can share her."

When Sam raised his eyebrow, Brendan merely smiled. "The sight of her lovely face. I was just telling her how long it had been for me since I had seen someone like her. Too long."

"You've been working too hard," Sam said. "Give us some details. We were just wondering what it was you're shipping this time around."

Brendan paused in the act of transferring a steaming steak to his plate. "Is that so?" He gave her an opaque look. "What a curious pair you two make. Sports equipment, if you can believe it."

"Really?" Sam asked, taking a bite. "Don't tell me you've got a cargo-hold full of basketballs."

"All varieties of recreational activities, or so I am told. I haven't inspected the merchandise."

Sam was looking at her now, head tilted. Probably because Brendan had been focused on her, completely, the entire time he conversed with his brother. Brendan was going to give it away like this.

"I loved going with you today," she told Sam quickly. "I hope you'll take me again."

Sam smiled slightly, though he seemed far from appeased. He wasn't stupid, and the subtext was fairly screaming. "Sure, subby. I like having you around."

Brendan needed a full minute to recover his silver tongue. "She speaks. This is new, yes?"

"Since earlier," Sam said smoothly. "So you see your worrying wasn't necessary. She's already getting better here."

"I still say she should come back with me." For once he turned and looked quite seriously at Sam. "What about

68

the people she left behind? Her family. For all you know she has a lover waiting for her, and here you are fucking her in a shithole cabin."

"That's enough," Sam said, his voice soft and menacing. "I let you give me a hard time, but I'm not going to let you disrespect her."

"You're not going to let *me* disrespect her? Oh, that's rich. She's a dirty little sex doll you found washed up, used up, half *dead*, and instead of sending her to people who might actually care about her, you dress her up in Amanda's old clothes and give her commands like she's a dog."

"Get out."

"Brother," he started.

"Now," Sam said with more than enough heat to show he meant it. If he had spoken to her that way, she would have cowered. Even now, she cowered.

Brendan took his time getting up. He wiped his mouth with a napkin and looked between her and his brother. She tried to ignore that, didn't let their gazes his meet. He would leave and she would be fine. He would leave, and she would go back to being Sam's recycled sex doll. She wanted to die.

"Fine, brother. Choose the girl, again. See if it turns out any better this time."

The door slammed shut behind Brendan, belying his coolly-spoken parting shot. Sam wouldn't look at her.

"Sir," she said. "Master?"

"Don't call me that."

She recoiled. He *was* mad at her.

"Please," she tried.

"My name's Sam. That's what you can call me. Say it. Say *please Sam*."

"Please, Sam," she whispered.

He looked at her then, but she almost wished he hadn't. She saw in his eyes disgust and fury. She saw herself turned away, cast off once again. The empty plastic doll left on the floor. Then he veiled his expression. "I'm going to go work. I need to just...you stay in the house. I mean it this time. Stay."

Hmm. Like a dog, indeed.

She stayed in her seat as he left the cabin and locked her inside. She really shouldn't mind. After all, she hadn't forgotten what they had done to her, but the more time that passed the quieter her fear.

Her sense of self had returned, but it wasn't a switch. Not off, then on, but something that stood and stretched and grew stronger with each kind word and gentle touch. She should be content to wait as his feet, to be put away when he no longer wanted her, to be shut out of his thoughts and emotions; she wasn't.

It was like she had been trapped at the bottom of the ocean in a hellish Atlantis. Then she had broken free and started swimming. Still deep, everything had been muted. She'd swum higher and higher and now she could see the surface, kicking furiously, dying for a single breath.

She didn't know what was at the top. She only knew that she had to get there.

Despite her uncertainty, she wouldn't disobey. She still worried that someone might be looking for her, and it was too dark to see. And even with her newfound strength, she didn't mind submission. There was a clarity here, a peace. She had only minded the way Brendan had spoken about her. She only worried he might be correct.

CHAPTER SEVEN

She woke in the dark, a book in her slack hands and a blanket over her knees. She must have drifted off, but where was Sam? Harsh breathing was too familiar, suddenly. A dark presence that taunted with its stillness.

Her throat tightened. "No."

"Yes," Brendan murmured. "See? You know me, even if you think you don't. You know who your master is."

The words made her breath catch, strange and meaningless to me. "Sam will come."

Hands enclosed her wrists, warm and firm. "What will he see? You submitting to me. Didn't he tell you about his last girlfriend?"

Oh God. *Sam.*

"He won't want anything to do with you then." Lips coasted over her shoulder, bringing goosebumps to her skin. "Where will you go? All alone in the woods. I'll take care of you."

It sounded like a threat. Would Sam hear her if she called to him?

"Come on, little girl." There was the pain she expected, almost wanted. Deserved. His fingers dug into my skin, pushing her down. "Fight me. I liked it when you fought."

But she didn't. She let him undress her, let him push her down onto her hands and knees, let him cup her breasts and squeeze. What could she do? Nothing, nothing at all. He was too strong, and she was too scared.

She imagined Sam working out there, just one building over. He would be tired by now but frustrated. Something had bothered him, so he kept sanding, cutting, stripping the wood with his hands. Then he would finally let go of whatever it was, through will or sheer exhaustion, and come inside to see his brother fucking his pet. Again.

She could do nothing. She *was* nothing. All the names that they called her—whore, slut, cum-hole—when had they become true? His fingers were inside her cunt, that part of her both exalted and feared. They worked in and out, drawing out pitiful moisture, making her ready.

She remembered arriving in a cold building. None of the girls would meet her eyes.

A sharp pain on her scalp and her head was pulled back. A voice against her ear. "My good girl. You'll be my good girl. It's what you want."

They'll never break me, she had promised to herself, silent and fierce. But what could she do?

Each time they beat her body, her mind would drift away. She could feel the pain, but it didn't matter so much in that empty house of hopelessness. This time, she felt the currents of his cruelty pull her out to sea. But she went somewhere else this time, to a place where color suffused the air, where sounds clashed in sharp harmony, where memories burst on her tongue like spices, rich and bittersweet.

My name is Melody Cole, and I was born in Syracuse, New York more years ago than I usually cared to admit. As a young child, I ran in a pack of girls, barefoot and wild, kicking up cold dry leaves behind us. We made a fort out of bed sheets and loose lumber that came down when the boys launched a full pillow assault. Soon enough my friends were drawn away from our tight circle by lopsided smiles and stammered invitations to the movies.

I wasn't, but not for lack of wanting. Too skinny to be hot, too shy to be noticed, I walked the same wooded trails alone. When I didn't get asked to prom, my mom set me up with the neighbors' college-aged son. He was surprisingly charming, and I put out for the first time that night.

I got my degree in business development and marketing from Penn State, and right about the time I decided I didn't need boys to make me happy, they discovered they liked my skinny body and aloofness. Dinner at a fabulous restaurant and coffee back at my place became standard Saturday night fare with whatever exec was passing through the office, but relationships took a backseat to my career.

It was a lonely existence and when one of my girlfriends needed a place to crash after breaking up with her boyfriend, I had been grateful for the company. We built a grown-up fort out of ice cream and sappy movies, swearing off pesky boys for good. But soon my friend grew restless, drawn away by five o'clock shadows and multiple orgasms.

Ever the follower, I tagged along with her to a munch, where a group of kinky folks got together and one of the Doms presented on the topic of informed consent. That Saturday I bailed on my scheduled date with the VP of Internal Development to go with her to the local kink club. Soon I was going a couple of nights a week, and several play partners had narrowed down to one, and next thing I knew, we had signed a power exchange contract and were picking out curtains.

I had been so sure of myself, smug in the certainty that I was doing the right thing. Powerful during the day and submissive at night—wasn't that every girl's fantasy? So I had everything.

Until my Dom and boyfriend told me I was too needy, too clingy. He was looking for a partner, not a pet. I needed to move out. Obedient to the end, I left, lost and needier than ever. The sweet contradiction of confidence and humility crumbled, leaving only a mess.

Things blurred after that. There was a gap in my memory, but it was a small tithe for all that had been returned to me.

I remembered, again, arriving in a cold building. I remembered that none of the girls would meet my eyes, and how that scared me worse than the guns and masks that had come before. I had sworn they would never break me.

I had been wrong. It had only been the shell of a woman who woke up here under Sam's reluctant guidance. Unable to speak, unable to remember, unable to even *think*.

Not anymore.

In a sudden motion, I jerked my head back. A crack sounded in my ear, followed by a pained groan. The impact hurt me too, but if there was one thing to be grateful for in all this, it was that my pain tolerance was practically a superpower at this point. When he tried to restrain me by my hair, I felt it rip from my scalp. When he grabbed hold of my wrist, I twisted hard, sending agony through my shoulder by breaking free in the same motion.

I shrugged off his attacks as if he were a butterfly flapping at my face. After fumbling with the lock, I flung open the lid of the trunk. A whip. That damned collar. *There.* The leather bundle unrolled, dropping the knife into my hand.

I whirled, and his look of shock sent dark satisfaction through me. I wondered if this is what the men had who hurt me had felt, the fear of his victim an aphrodisiac to violence.

"I was worried about you," he said. "Worried we'd gone too far."

His words distracted me. I had suspected he was involved with the men who had held me prisoner, but this was as close to an admission as I was likely to get.

"Why? Why would you do it?" My voice cracked.

His lids lowered. "Trust me, you wanted it."

I should have expected a sick, blame-the-victim excuse. "I guess that helps you sleep at night."

"To be honest, I haven't slept that much lately." He paused. "Like I said, I'd been worried."

Confused, the knife lowered a bit. He helped men who tortured and raped women, but he worried about us? I would have thought he was batshit crazy except that he seemed perfectly lucid, and definitely regretful.

A squeak at the door was my only warning. I scrambled for some way to explain, but it was too late. Sam took one look at me and then crossed the room to tackle Brendan. They fought like wild animals, teeth bared and bodies tangling. Blows exchanged almost too fast to count, too vicious to hope Sam wouldn't be hurt.

They were lost to their rage, and I knew it was more than this, more than me. It was the woman that came before me, it was years of competing and bitterness, it was being born to a sibling he hated but loving him anyway.

"Stop," I whispered. "Stop fighting. Please."

I had become irrelevant, standing in the corner. I wanted to make them stop but short of running into the fray myself or stabbing one of them, I didn't know how to grab their attention. Beside me, a long single-tail lay coiled where I'd pulled it from the trunk. The sight of it normally struck fear in me, but this time there was only sick calm.

I picked it up and tentatively snapped the whip. The writhing mass of pissed off males moved out of the way, and the leather slapped wood instead. This time I hit Sam on the back. It didn't slow them down, but when the whip licked the side of Brendan's neck, he yelped.

They fought still, but the air had shifted. Sensing weakness, smelling blood, an animal would go for the kill.

Instead, they pulled their punches, aimed for sturdier places, blood bonds conquering bloodlust once again.

With a final surge, Sam pinned Brendan face down on the floor in a twisted imitation of the way Brendan had once held me. Though subdued, he didn't look at all submissive.

"You bastard," Sam said in a low voice that filled the room. "How dare you come into my house. Touch *my* girl."

Brendan's laugh sent shivers through me. "You think she's yours?"

The cool confidence in his voice seemed to give Sam pause. He eased off a bit. "I don't care what she said. What you did to seduce her. You knew she was mine. You knew I wanted her to be."

Brendan's shoulders slumped into the floor, and he finally looked defeated even as Sam stood. Brendan staggered up, wiping a trickle of blood from his mouth. "You're right about that. I knew exactly how much it would hurt to see me with her. Maybe that's why I did it. Fuck." He put a fist to his forehead, and he looked so oddly pained that it caused an answering pang in my stomach.

Even Sam seemed surprised. He eased off and leaned, panting, against the wall. "Get the hell out. Don't ever come back."

Brendan stood. He looked like he was about to fall over, but he caught himself. "Fine. I'll leave. I know I fucked this up. If she wants to stay here, she can. But I was right about one thing." The look he gave me caught my breath with its intensity. "She doesn't belong here."

He left, and the door slammed shut followed by the sound of his heavy, uneven footsteps leading away. Then there was only the sound of my breathing, overshadowed by Sam's harsh breaths.

I wrapped my arms around myself, but the chill was too deep. "I didn't want him."

He slanted me a look but didn't say anything. His chest heaved, muscles bulging from the white undershirt he wore. Already a bruise was forming on his cheek.

"Please, Sam." My voice shook. "I *am* yours. That's what I wanted."

"And what do you want now?"

I swallowed. "I don't know. I just know... I remembered who I am."

"Do you?" His voice lowered. "So you've got a place of your own. A family?"

"Something like that. A job, anyway." A sterile apartment. Shallow friendships.

His gaze sharpened on the floor. He approached, not looking at me, and knelt before it. The collar lay discarded on the floor. He picked it up with a reverence that made my heart pound.

I thought... I hoped...

His head was bowed. "How did you know what was in here?"

"I'm sorry. I looked in there when you were out. I know I shouldn't have."

He sighed. "You don't belong here."

"No, please. Don't send me away. I don't know... what's going to happen with all that. But I know I care about you."

A coarse laugh escaped him. "You care about me. That's not exactly what I want from you."

I knelt beside him, staring at the collar in his hand. "What do you want?"

"I want you." His fingers curled around the worn leather. "But what about your life out there?"

I bent at the waist until my cheek rested on his knee. "I've been gone for weeks. For months. It can wait for one more night." His hand stroked me hair, giving me the strength to continue. "I know I have to go back, but show me what it would be like to be yours."

He ran a hand through his hair. "I'm not sure I can do

77

it like that. I'm not sure it will be enough for me."

Proving I could be just as selfish as any man, any master, I said, "Then do it for me."

I had been so sure that this was it, that I would be happy here forever, if he only wanted me. But my memories were a siren song, thoughts of what might have been a sweet and sudden obsession. Like Odysseus, I wanted someone to tie me to the ship, to help me resist because I was too weak to do it on my own. I wanted Sam to keep me, to tie me down and fuck me, if only for tonight.

CHAPTER EIGHT

I lay on his bed, face down. There were other places we could have played: the spanking bench in the workroom, since presumably it wouldn't be a gift for his brother anymore, or even the beach where we had played before. But his bed was soft, his scent soothing.

With my ears plugged and eyes blindfolded, I was adrift before he even touched me. But when he did—ahh, I was oversensitive but with a desperate, almost painful need for more. More, harder, deeper, and that was only his fingers on my sex, sending waves of silky pleasure through me.

Even when his hands were gone, I floated on the echoes—perfect. And the first light thuds of his palm on my skin were even better. He took his time, warmed me up, built my arousal so hot and so sharp that all I knew was wanting and all I could think was *more*.

I strained against the bed, searching for that rhythm, that extra bit of pressure that would push me over. A sharp slap on the inside of my thigh put a stop to that— the light sting reminded me that what I felt wasn't really pain, that this wasn't a beating, not really.

Despite his self-proclaimed status as a sadist, his assertions that he was just as bad as those other men, I knew he was just like me. I was submissive, and he dominant, but we both wanted this frenzy. For us sex wasn't a train but a roller coaster, and the fear as we approached the top only made the drop sweeter.

There was a wash of cool air on my burning skin before the kiss of a flogger touched me. He was thorough, marking me with heat, branding me with sensation. *Please, oh please.*

After a pause, he started the whip. At first it was an extension of what came before, a continuation of feeling and arousal, but slowly it grew, turned harsh. I tensed, but that only made it worse. Each slash ripped into my skin, tore tears from my eyes because this wasn't meant to be sexy. It was supposed to hurt, and it did, and what had I done wrong? Should I have been more still, more quiet… no, I had been silent, all this time.

Maybe he wanted some noise from me, a symbol of my slavery, proof of my pain. Was this the payment for this thing he hadn't really wanted to do? Or punishment for leaving him after all?

In the end, it didn't matter. The cruel bite of the whip pulled soft cries from me, until soft kisses rained down on my forehead, my cheek, washing away the sting of betrayal. The props were the same, the choreography familiar, but Sam didn't open my skin and leave me in a cell. He was different, wasn't he? He had to be different.

The bed dipped, soft flesh pressed my lips. In the universal command of a man to a woman—please me, and I'll take care of you. More primitive, more painful: please me, and I won't hurt you. I answered him in the only way I could, with the flick of my tongue and the heat of my mouth and the tears that leaked out of my eyes, dampening the fabric of the blindfold.

He stroked my hair but didn't stop his slow slide in and out, validating my feelings but rendering them irrelevant. This was what I wanted, to feel low and cherished at the same time. He tasted like lust and violence, like salt and sweat. His cock was thick in my mouth, hard and soft and powerful, and I filled with a special kind of joy that only came from service.

Then he was gone, and there were hands on my back, the tender flesh of my ass, my sex. He was everywhere, he surrounded me, and how, how could I leave him? How could I give this up, when I had only just learned its comforts?

His knees nudged my legs apart, a heavy hand on my hips tilted me back.

"Please," I whispered. "Sam." Then I cringed, expecting a blow, still broken.

He took the plugs out of my ears, and oddly, everything grew quiet, expectant. "It's okay," he whispered. "You're doing great."

"I don't know... how to be. I want to please you."

"You please me, Melody. Just by accepting me, that I want to restrain you, to give you pain. By trusting me, after all you've been through. That pleases me more than I can say."

He pushed inside me, slowly, steadily, inexorably to the hilt. My mouth opened in a silent gasp. There wasn't pain now, not even pleasure, only fullness and feeling and a reckless kind of devotion that can only come from intimacy.

Pulling back out, he paused. "I don't think I can hold back."

I made fists in my restraints, then went slack, allowing his hard use of me—no, wanting it. Needing it, because I wasn't a fragile woman nor was I a slave. For me consent would always be like fire, warm and necessary and untouchable. This was all I had: wanting a man and having him want me back, *yes*.

"Then don't," I said. "Take me."

Even so, the force of his next thrust took me by surprise, turned me inside out. He didn't use me like an object, because a thing didn't need to be mastered. He didn't use me like a slave, because a slave didn't need to feel wanted. He used me like a woman, hungry and desperate. I was tossed on the sea of his lust, torn apart by the onslaught of my orgasm, and gently floated back to shore by his low, rumbling groan of release.

With an air of regret, he pulled out of me and undid the restraints, massaging each limb and kissing the faint red marks left behind. I didn't feel like a slave but like royalty, constrained by my position but pampered, cherished. Loved.

"Thank you," I said, luxuriating in the soft-worn sheets and post-orgasmic rush.

He only smiled, his hair still askew and skin damp. The intensity from earlier hadn't abated entirely, instead it was carefully banked within the care he gave me. Even the glass of water he handed me was a symbol of his possession of me—and a stark reminder of the first time I had seen him.

I had knelt before him, and he had hated it then. I hadn't understood it, but now I knew it was because it had been meaningless. That blind subservience had been a mockery of the submission he wanted from me. My lazy, sated smile was more potent devotion than I had ever given those other men.

He sat down beside me and put my hand between his. "What's next?"

The words were spoken lightly, but I swallowed hard. "Don't ask me that."

His smile was a little sad. "Giving orders already, subby? I should spank you for that."

"Please. Make me stay here. I won't disobey you."

"I should keep you chained to my bed, is that it? Sure, it's tempting, but I don't want to be just like those other guys, keeping you here because you're too afraid to fight for something better."

"It's different."

"I see that." His expression turned rueful. "I'm afraid

82

you're the one who doesn't."

"I want to be with you." I begged him with my eyes. Just this once, give into me. Just once, let me be in control. Make me yours, and I'll obey you forever.

But it didn't work that way—I knew it didn't.

"You won't make me stay?" I said, knowing the answer, fearing it.

His expression was opaque as he said, "I won't make you leave."

He would let me stay here, but he wouldn't stop me from leaving. I almost hated him for a sick, unhappy moment. A caged bird always tries to get out, but a good owner keeps it safe. Why wouldn't he help me? If an animal lives too long in captivity, it won't be able to survive on its own. Humans were supposed to be more advanced than animals, more *humane*, but this just seemed cruel.

But I wasn't Sam's pet. He hadn't collared me.

It was time for me to go home.

CHAPTER NINE

The air was thick with smog and dense with noise, brimming with the refuse of people crammed too close. Breathing on the crowded city sidewalk was only marginally better than the small aircraft, where the sketchy climate control had left me alternately shivering and sweating my way across the ocean.

It was surprisingly easy to sneak into the US undetected. I had heard all of the stories about hiding in one-hundred degree trucks across the border, but apparently it helped that my speech was so clearly American or that I was Caucasian. Of course, it also hadn't hurt that Sam had spotted me several thousand dollars and the name of a shipping business happy to take on an extra hundred and twenty pounds of cargo. They even helped me slip undetected through the airport, although their own asses would have been on the line if I'd been caught.

Now I was on my own, in this city that had been home, and wondering why, why? What was so special about here? All these people rushing around, and I had nothing to do. Nowhere to go. I had a vague recollection of a white-walled apartment. A slightly stronger memory of a desk where I had spent most of my days and many of my nights, offering subservience to a corporate master alongside thousands of other drones.

But I couldn't just walk back into the apartment or show up at work. I had been gone for so long, probably reported missing at some point, but by whom I didn't know. I didn't even have keys or any identification at all.

A woman jostled me, shooting back a dirty look before she resumed her path and her phone conversation. I looked down at myself, wondering what she thought of me. I wore another light dress from Sam's endless arsenal, this one a light pink with white piping around the edges. It had felt feminine when I put it on. Now its bare arms and short hem felt perverse, like I was on display as some sex object.

Ironic, considering.

I rubbed my hands along my arms, trying to ward off the chills. It didn't matter what I looked like because no one was really looking. I could fade away, and no one would notice. No one would care. Faced with such cold indifference, the cruel attention of the men who had hurt me took on a softer light.

Lifting my hand, I hailed a cab. The dark-skinned man behind the wheel leered at the scoop of my neckline. "Where to, miss?"

"The nearest police station, please."

His eyes widened for a second of concern, before his lids lowered to complacency once again. It only took a few minutes and a couple of turns before we pulled up at a run-down looking building. Precinct 45, it said.

The little monitor was blank. "How much do I owe you?" I asked.

"It's on the house," he said gruffly, not turning around.

Embarrassed by his help, by my obvious need of it, I murmured my thanks and left the cab. For endless minutes, I stood outside the police station, deliberating. Did I have to go inside? There was nowhere else to go. And what would I tell them? I had nothing to offer but the truth.

A man stopped in front of me, wearing a rumpled suit and holding a steaming cup of coffee. I didn't have time to be afraid, because his posture was clearly so reluctant, as if he hoped I would walk away before he had to intervene. I looked up into his hard face and kind eyes and burst into tears, overwhelmed by the growing certainty that this was my life now and that it would always be this lonely.

He ushered me inside the station and into a small room with a table and a few chairs. His name was Detective Hines, he said, but he would find someone who could take my statement. Probably someone female, I understood.

"No, please." I didn't want to face the knowing in another woman's eyes. The sympathy laced with relief that it wasn't her who had been hurt that way.

Though it was clear he'd rather be anywhere but here, he agreed. Notepad in hand, he began asking questions. The first few were straightforward: my name, my age, what I remembered of my life. The *before* was implied.

There was a gap in my memory then, around the time it happened. Not just in the immediate moment when I was taken, but in those weeks, months, who knew how long? It was like squinting into a muddy whirlpool—it made me dizzy to even try.

Talking about my time in captivity was harder. My memory there was spotty as well, but I remembered more than enough details to get the point across. Detective Hines was thin-lipped through my more graphic descriptions but all business, without any of the pity that would have made me fall apart all over again.

I described the day when everything had changed. They were moving us. It was clearly sudden, not well planned. We were outside, naked but not chained. In the mayhem, another man came and told us to follow him. I didn't recognize him, but we were like sheep—we all would have jumped off a cliff just to obey. People were shouting; I was so scared. I hid in a bush, cowering, waiting for someone to find me and punish me. When no one did, I gained enough awareness to realize this was my chance. I ran.

"I just… kept running, until I reached a town and they gave me these clothes and helped me find a plane that would bring me back." I spread my hands, pretending they didn't shake, wishing I could look at him while I lied. "So that's what happened."

He had stopped writing during the last, and when I dared to glance up, his expression made it clear that he knew it was bullshit. His voice was even. "That was a pretty lucky break, then."

"Yes." My eyes fell shut, then I looked at him directly. "What happened to me was horrible, but I can honestly say I was lucky after that."

He tapped the pen to the notepad, clearly considering. He nodded, as if he'd made a decision. "All right. If that's what happened, all right. I'll need to look into this of course, but without any specifics about where you were, I doubt we'll find much. Still, we'll definitely investigate your case. That might be the best clue we have to finding them…and helping those other women."

I swallowed against a gnawing guilt that I had made it home when they hadn't. "Anything I can do to help."

He grunted with something like approval before flagging down a couple of younger cops and barking out orders. The detective escorted me personally to a hotel, where I would have to stay until they had gone over my apartment once again. They had also taken some of my DNA to reinstate me as the real Melody Cole, since my fingerprints had ever been taken and apparently I had no immediate family to confirm.

That part was depressing. I had been nervous about the prospect of some unremembered boyfriend or even husband who would expect my love and loyalty, when I had none to give. But I had been hoping for someone, a mother, a brother, someone to help ease the way.

I stared at the thin walls of the hotel, sat on the thin

bedspread and breathed the thin air. What was a home without people you loved but an empty box anyway? Detective Hines had paused before he'd left and said, "It will get better." But how could it when every second was another one without Sam? I finally allowed myself to think about him, allowing myself to mourn the loss I recognized in his face at the end.

What would he think of the city? Too congested, maybe. I thought he would like Detective Hines.

What would he say if he were here? *Spread your legs, subby.*

With a private smile, I slipped beneath the covers and obeyed his imaginary commands.

Touch yourself.

No, slower.

We have all night.

There was probably a psychology student somewhere writing a salacious thesis on women like me. Abused, confused, we couldn't even help it. We paid with sex, we coped with sex, everything was sex to a poor liberated slave. But my body didn't care about political correctness, and my mind wasn't too broken up over it either. This was Sam's gift to me: my sexuality returned, pleasure sharpened.

The timbre of his voice reverberated deep inside me as my fingers stroked my clit, like touching a memory. I climaxed to the brush of his breath, the ache of his hands, the warmth of his praise.

I came back to myself as the AC switched off, casting me in a bittersweet silence.

CHAPTER TEN

"Are you sure you don't want to go? You don't have to play. Just have a few drinks." Anya frowned. "It's been two months already."

Two months of working at this job, though I hadn't yet figured out why it was so important that we made the regional top sales lists. Two months of returning home to a cold, empty apartment. But the thought of going out into a crowd was even worse.

I stood up from my desk and stretched. "I'll take a rain check."

I still didn't remember how I had ended up in the hands of those men or why I had been targeted. For all I knew, it could have been a random drugging at a kink club just like the one she was always pushing me to accompany her to.

"You need to relax. Have a good time. You can meet a guy who can give you one." She gave me a suggestive smile. "What's the worst that can happen?"

Rape and torture, though I wouldn't say so. I wouldn't risk my friendship, however two-dimensional it was, with Anya, when she had been so willing, even eager, to reconnect with me. Everyone else I met in the hallways had avoided me since I got back, as if my presumed psychological trauma were contagious.

"Look." Her face softened while her eyes took on a strange glint. "You can tell me what happened to you. Maybe it will help you work it out."

There was something about the way she focused on me, her posture...

"I don't think so," I said. "It's kind of hard to talk about."

She laid her hand over mine. "I know, but I won't judge you. No matter what they did to you. Seriously."

A shiver ran through me as I recognized her expression: anticipation. Like she might get off on what I told her. No, that couldn't be right. Probably just some sort of clinical paranoia shit, keeping anyone from getting too close. She wanted to help me.

And I did want to be wrapped up tight somewhere, safe somehow. Maybe a Dom could give me that. The thought of being under a stranger's control made me nervous, even though I knew that not every man was like them.

I glanced down the hallway to make sure no one was nearby. "Well, it's hard for me to imagine being with a man... that way. Not just sex, but giving over my power like that. And to someone I don't know or trust. To be honest, it's really scary."

"Exactly! You'll be afraid as long as you don't do it.

Fear of the unknown. You need to face your fears. Once you find an awesome Dom, one who knows how to treat you right, you'll be fine."

I was skeptical but nervous about disagreeing with her outright. I may have been uneasy enough to keep the specifics of what happened to me, especially regarding Sam, to myself, but I was lonely enough not to cut off contact with her completely.

"I'm sorry," I said. "I'm really just… not ready."

She turned away but not before I saw her roll her eyes. God, I wished I could be back to normal. Back then we had gone out, had a couple martinis, woken up in strange beds in pricey high-rise condos, and compared bruises the next day at work. It was a good time, wasn't it?

I shook off the feeling that I was being watched in the parking garage. It was a leftover feeling from being held captive, I told myself. Not real.

Dropping my bag in the entryway, I stood in the middle of my apartment. A chic blue sofa sat in front of a flat-screen television. A fake white daisy sat in the windowsill. Though I had quickly fallen into the routine of my work, I had never felt comfortable here. The cool air felt stale, the 600-threadcount sheets dusty.

Maybe I should move, though the thought of packing up all this impersonal stuff made me glum. Maybe I could find a cute little house. Something with trees, where I could see the stars. Somewhere I could breathe again. That brightened my mood, even though I'd have a painful commute.

I wandered into the bathroom, brushed my fingertips

across the expensive cosmetics. I had found them unopened in the cabinets, as if I'd been stockpiling for the nuclear holocaust with organic astringent. The countertops had been empty... I paused. There hadn't even been a toothbrush.

So what had I used before I'd been taken?

A chill ran through me, but it was just that overzealous AC again. Not like the cool moist air by the water, the smell of trees and rain...

She doesn't belong here. I shivered, as if I heard Brendan's voice right beside me.

As if unlocked, more disembodied words played in the same dreaded voice, the sound hollow like a lone wolf's howl. *Don't you love me? Don't you trust me? I'm doing this for you, not just me. You want to be the best submissive. I want that for you too. I'll be so proud of you.*

I do want to be a good submissive, came my fervent voice. *I just don't understand why you can't train me. What will they do that you can't?*

You don't understand. This is hardcore, not the kind of thing we can do in public or in my condo.

Well, I don't see how I can leave my job for a whole month.

You won't work when you're with me, anyway. Stop being selfish, Melody.

God, that was creepy. And not real at all. Brendan had never said any of that to me. My mind had taken my darkest insecurities and deepest hopes and set them to a damn scary tune. I felt bad about leaving Sam to return to my life here—that had to be where this was coming from. But that's all it was: a soundtrack to a nightmare.

Just forget about all of that, Anya had told me over

lunch while I stared out the window, seeing only glass and concrete and smog. Then she scolded me for not paying attention when she was helping me. A rueful smile tilted my lips. If anyone was going to scold me, I'd rather it were Sam. At least he would give me a spanking afterward.

That was exactly the kind of thing that would set her off again.

Sam had abused my weakened state, she said. That wasn't real BDSM.

Well, he had abused something all right. My ass.

Traumatic bonding, she had read online somewhere.

We had both agreed that sounded kinky.

Well, she was probably right about my mind being all messed up. But maybe it didn't matter. If I wanted to be with Sam and he liked me this way, it should be enough. Every day, I believed a little bit more. It could be enough.

I had been so confused when I first got back, lost. Everything had seemed foreign at the beginning. Now I examined the apartment with new eyes, like an investigator looking for clues. Who am I? And why would anyone want to live in this sterilized bubble of an apartment?

Clothes hung in the closet, neat. The cabinets were stacked with toiletries and linens, everything so orderly. I remembered this as my apartment; it just didn't feel *lived* in.

I went to the fridge where some cut fruit and a jar of milk sat in the front. It was otherwise empty. No clue as to what I had eaten before, no rotten telltale food.

Someone must have cleaned it out when I had gone missing. That was smart, not creepy. A missing persons report had been filed, police had been through here.

Despite my own vigorous assurances, I sat on the couch with my arms wrapped around my waist, hunched over as if invisible enemies might storm through the walls. I couldn't just sit here. I needed to talk to someone.

Not Anya, because I had definitely used up as much support time as she could spare. Besides I wasn't looking forward to another lecture on how a random Dom could beat me into healing. Been there, done that.

I flipped through the numbers on my phone. My old cell phone had disappeared when I did and never been found. This was a new fancy thing that I couldn't really figure out, and the only numbers on here were Anya's and a few other people's I barely knew. As I stared at the cluttered screen, the phone vibrated and rang. I jumped, startled, and didn't relax much when I saw who was calling.

"Hello?"

"Hello, Ms. Cole. This is Detective Hines."

Willy had called every week since I got back, but it had only been a few days since his last check-in. What could be wrong? I smoothed my hands over my skirt and told myself to get a grip. "What is it?"

"I finally got your old phone records here. They were sealed up real tight. Are you sure you don't know anyone who'd have the motive or influence to do something like that?"

"No, I... " That was the problem. I couldn't

remember everything. This life seemed so flat, so empty. Had I really lived like this? "I think I'm just your average girl."

"An average girl with a boyfriend, looks like. One number appears pretty often, especially leading up to your disappearance. Know anyone by the name of Pike? Brendan Pike?"

A rushing sound filled my ears, drowning out his next words. "I don't know," I mumbled. "I'm sorry. I don't know."

The phone slipped from my fingers. Hines's voice, tinny and small now, buzzed from the ground, and all I could think was: I really don't belong here. I had to get out. Grabbing my purse, I took the elevator downstairs but paused in front of the doorman.

I would have passed him every day, but he gave me a blank look. "Can I help you?"

"Listen, I know this is going to sound strange, but I was gone for a while and I'm a little… well, I live in apartment 9A. Did anyone used to come visit me? Maybe regularly. Like… a guy?" Well, didn't I just sound like a stupid little slut? That thought hit a little close to home.

He glanced at the door. "I'm sorry, ma'am, but I'm new here, so I couldn't really say."

"Ah. While I was, uh, gone, someone cleared out my fridge. I was wondering who might have done that? Or—" I waved my hand. "—had access?"

"Let me check with the building owner." He got on a wall phone. "Yes, sir. Sorry to bother you. There's a woman here asking about who had access to her place.

Yeah, 9A. Okay, I'll tell her, sir."

He hung up and turned to me. "That was the building owner. He says if you can wait in your apartment, he'll come up personally and answer any questions for you."

That wasn't supposed to sound threatening. I was being paranoid. The doorman's attention had already wandered away, even as I stood in front of him.

No way in hell was I going back upstairs.

I hit the pavement, letting the cold weather and my vigorous pace steal my breath. Finally I looked around. I recognized this intersection; I was only a few blocks away from the club where Anya was. I didn't know if she could help me, but I didn't have anyone else to turn to, anywhere else to go.

My knowledge of the city was like a dream, the more I grasped for it, the farther it slipped away. Instead, I allowed myself to wander. I turned a corner and saw a crowd of people in front of a building with bold lettering: *El Diablo*. Recognition flashed, and I knew I had found it.

At the door, the bouncer looked at me, his expression impassive, and then let me in ahead of the line. Still edgy, I slipped inside among the throngs of people. Most of them wore regular club gear, black shirts and tight skirts. A few people wore more obvious bondage clothes, but here in the front there was only drinks and dancing. Play was downstairs, I remembered.

I skated the edge of the bar until I saw Anya's blonde mane of hair in a smoky corner. She was chatting with a cute young guy, and judging from his hunched position and glazed eyes, she was practicing her Domme moves again. Her eyes widened in surprise as she saw me approach. "You decided to come!"

"I'm sorry to barge in like this, but I need to talk to you. Something's happened."

"Let's talk later. Come on downstairs. There's a guy who would be perfect for you."

"Please, Anya." My throat grew tight. "I'm scared."

She stood and put her hand around my waist. "Oh, baby. You have nothing to worry about, a pretty girl like you." She gave me a once-over, taking in the cream-colored business suit I still wore. She frowned. "I wish you would have changed before coming." Then she brightened. "But he'll have you out of that in no time."

I felt like I was drowning. The bodies rocking me, air growing thin. "What's happening?"

She leaned in close. "Trust me. He knows what you like."

How would she know? Her insistence flayed open the fear I had kept so tightly under wraps these past two months. I had a premonition that if I went downstairs, I may never come back up.

"If you're sure this guy is right for me," I said, striving for casual, "maybe I'll give him a try. Let me just freshen up."

She looked like she wanted to come with me, and she'd have the perfect excuse. We used to go into the bathroom together and share dirt on the guys we were with. She always carried a flask in her purse, the hard stuff, and we'd take a shot of liquid courage before going back out.

"I just need a minute," I said quickly. "I need to redo my make-up before I meet someone."

"Okay," she agreed. "Do your lipstick at least. And hurry back."

In the restroom, I leaned on the sink, staring into my bloodshot eyes. I looked a mess. Anyone could see I wasn't up for playing. I probably wouldn't even pass the monitor's inspection. Why did she want me to play with someone so badly?

The door opened and I tensed, thinking it was Anya come to check up on me. But instead a slim woman in a black sheath and high heels came in, laughing at something on her way inside.

My breath caught in my throat. I knew her from somewhere, from another lifetime. I didn't know her name, but I knew she cried at the first touch of pain, and then grew quiet when she fell into subspace. I knew the thing she feared most was needles.

I gaped at her as she went into a stall, waited dumbly until she came back out. She noticed me as she washed her hands.

She smiled. "Hi."

"Um, hi. I'm sorry, but you seem really... familiar."

"Oh, I remember you. You're talking again." She looked radiant, and as unaffected as if we were swapping stories about a day spa.

"Right. So. What...how did you get back?"

"The same as you, I suppose. When you're ready. When we're done."

When we're done—like turkeys in the oven. And she was *okay* with it?

"I don't understand," I said. "They shouldn't have...I didn't want that. I hated it there. *You* hated it there."

Her face drew into a small frown, looking tragic and haunted and beautiful. "It's not about what I like. I want to serve my Master."

Her makeup was flawless, her up-do classy. The hem of her dress exposed long, shapely legs adorned with leather cuffs. Complete with a placid expression, she was a kinky Stepford wife.

"Um. I gotta go," I muttered, angry and confused.

"It was great to see you again," I heard her say before the door swung shut.

I edged around the crowd and pushed out an emergency exit that I knew from my many visits here wouldn't set off an alarm. The stench of the street was a relief to me. I leaned against the concrete wall, catching my breath. The atmosphere in there had been stifling, Anya's pushiness unsettling, but that slave was terrifying. Was that supposed to be me?

The door squealed open behind me, and I startled, thinking Anya had followed me. Instead it was the bouncer from the front. "You need to leave," he said.

I glanced around the small alley. "Oh, I'm sorry. I'm going, I promise."

He shook his head. "Not here. You need to leave the club. The city. It isn't safe for you here."

He knows. "How?"

With a shrug, he said, "That's above my pay grade. You were marked for the program. Then you went away, and now you're back except..."

"Except what?"

"You're still you."

"Just tell me something. Do you know someone named Brendan?"

He gave me a strange look. "Don't you?"

"I don't remember," I whispered. "Please tell me. I can't remember what I need to know, and it's killing me."

There was a long pause, where I knew he was debating the risk to himself.

Finally he said, "Some girls want to be more submissive. Hell, most submissives do. Comes with the mindset." He shrugged. "Or even if they don't want it. They go off, get a little training, and come back to their lives here, but now they're the best subs in the scene. Everyone wants them, but they're completely devoted to their Dom."

I choked on the words. "And that happened to me?"

"You were Brendan's girl, and then you were marked. What do you think?"

"I think I brought this on myself." My survival instincts told me to run, but a growing horror chained me to the spot. Through everything that had happened, my helplessness had been my treasured safety blanket. Oh, the regular stand-bys of shame and guilt still visited me on occasion, but as long as it was all forced, I could absolve myself them. But if I had ever consented to that... then I was the monster.

I swallowed thickly. "What do I do?"

"Well, that's the thing. Every girl that's ever come back is different. To be honest... they seem pretty happy. But not you. I don't see how they can let you go around, asking questions, stirring up trouble. It's not going to look good. Something's gonna have to be done. That's why I said, you need to leave." With that he reentered the club, leaving me in the cold.

I walked briskly into the shadows with nowhere to go. The club had turned out to be a snake's nest; I was lucky to have gotten out alive. I couldn't go back to my apartment, where Brendan was possibly waiting for me. I couldn't go back to work tomorrow either and face Anya and my suspicions that she had been involved in my abduction—that she had tried again tonight.

I stood on an unfamiliar street corner and allowed myself to be jostled to and fro. What was I doing here? This wasn't reclaiming my life. My friends had betrayed me; I felt so alone. This hadn't been a life at all.

I never should have left Sam, but I could rectify my error. I had to flee somewhere, and the islands had never sounded more appealing. I took out as much cash as I could from an ATM and boarded the first flight south.

CHAPTER ELEVEN

The soft island breeze was a balm to my fear. It was sunny when I stepped out of the small airport, the brightness barely dimmed by the rain that pattered on the window of the cab. I arrived in a small building. This village was the farthest outskirts of civilization, and this grungy bar was at its center.

A bell tinkled as I pushed inside. My heart thudded—what if someone here had worked with Brendan? They might recognize me. But the bar was mostly empty, and no one looked very curious about a woman in a crumpled business suit and Manolo Blahniks.

The bartender had a face of leather and scruff, his eyes only visible in small red-black pools.

"Que pasa?" he asked.

I had fretted on the plane—how would I find Sam's place? "Hi, I'm looking for someone with a boat. Un barco?"

"Forty dolares," he said flatly.

I fumbled with the native currency I had exchanged at the last international airport.

"No," he said. "American dolares."

After handing over the requested amount, he left through the back door. I glanced awkwardly at the other patrons, one of whom seemed asleep—at least I hoped that's what he was. It seemed I should follow the bartender, so I edged around the bar and exited through the same door. He was already several paces away, walking toward the water where a man sat on a small boat.

They spoke rapidly together, too fast for me to understand, as I caught up. The bartender gestured me inside the boat. "Sam..." Well, that was deflating, to realize I didn't know his last name. Except I did, because now I knew Brendan's. "Sam Pike." I flipped through my little dictionary. "Un hombre. Cabina... solitario."

He didn't react to my words except to gesture me inside.

For all I knew, they could be taking me captive, leading me straight to Brendan's men. I could imagine them bragging about it back in the bar later: *she didn't even put up a fight!* I told myself, again, that all men weren't bad, but the truth was I was in the middle of nowhere. Home wasn't safe for me anymore. I needed to find Sam and hope he would take me back. Oh please let him take me back.

Gingerly, I climbed inside the small green boat. The man in the boat barely glanced at me but when I was seated, he tapped the engine with a wrench, and it sputtered to life. Well, that was a relief. The sight of the oars at the bottom didn't escape me.

Cold sea spray lashed my face as he picked up speed.

I glanced nervously at the tree-lined beaches, all alike and unfamiliar. "Do you know where we're going?" I asked dumbly. "I'm sorry, do you speak English?"

I thought he wasn't going to answer, but then he said, "Carpintero, eh?"

The dictionary, carpintero... carpenter!

"Yes, that's right!" Relief swept through me, solidified when I sighted the pebble beach with what looked like a large rocky overgrowth—the cave. They must have figured out where I needed to go from my bumbling attempts. Or maybe we were just the only Americanos in the vicinity.

He cut the engine, and we drifted until the hull batted against the rocky floor. Taking off my shoes, I jumped into the shallow water. *I'm coming, Sam.*

"Oh, did you need payment too?" I turned back, but the man had already pushed it away with an oar in the water. As I watched, he clanged the wrench on the engine casing and sped away, landing a fresh spray of water over my suit.

I cut the soles of my feet to ribbons along the beach. I glanced with longing and anticipation at the beach. There was a parallel to our play, that the payoff was all the sweeter when I had paid from my body.

Or maybe I was just giddy. *Oh, Sam.*

I passed the clearing where he had felled the tree and followed the path toward his cabin. The rain had stopped, but everything was wet with it, light reflecting off slippery branches, leaves quivering with weighty drops, everything bright with anticipation.

There it was, so small and humble and proud at once. My heart swelled. This was home.

I knocked on the door with abandon. "Sam!"

When he didn't answer, I checked the knob and went inside. "It's me, Melody. Where are you?"

Everything looked like I had left it, except the black trunk was missing. I spared a quick frown for the empty corner before checking the two bedrooms, the bathroom, the kitchen—all empty. He must be in the workroom. Stumbling through the back door, I ran across the yard and burst in on the room.

The discordant piles of furniture had disappeared; in its place stood a bedroom... of sorts.

A bed was clearly the focal point, built with wood of rich caramel. There was a side table, a drawer. And beside those ordinary things, I recognized the spanking bench. A few other standalone pieces, whose overall shapes I recognized from the dungeon that I remembered from my time in slavery, all designed to hurt.

Blood raced through my veins, and for a moment, I was back there, running through the woods, away, away. A man's voice calling, "Melody!" Who had been chasing me?

I had told Sam when I remembered my life back home. He had said, *You please me, Melody*. But I had never told him my name. Confusion and dread knotted in my stomach.

What had I done?

In a trance, I crept toward the bed, as if the intricate carving in the headboard would have my answer. A nymph stood by a river, her hands covering her ears, mouth open. Her expression was a mixture of horror and fear, like a reflection of my own heart.

"That's Echo," said a voice behind me.

I whirled around to see Sam come inside and casually close the door. He was wearing a red plaid shirt, hung open to reveal a white undershirt, and his well-worn jeans. How could he look so beautiful and ordinary at the same time? He had brought the smell of the woods in with him, and I realized he must have been out for a hike, perhaps chopping another tree. My sweet, harmless lumberjack—how wrong I had been.

"Sam, no," I whispered.

He sat down on a stool, hooked his boots in the rungs. "Some people think she slept with Zeus, but that's not true."

"It's mythology. None of it's true."

"Don't interrupt," he said mildly. "But Echo didn't sleep with Zeus, or maybe she did, but that's not what got her in trouble. It was because she helped him go off and rape all those little mortal girls by distracting his wife. It was Hera who put the curse on her. Echo can't speak unless spoken to. She can only repeat what others have said."

I hugged myself, gripping the wet, ragged silk of my suit. "Why are you doing this?"

"The story has a sad ending. Echo falls in love with a man, Narcissus, but he doesn't want her." Sam slanted me a look. "Obviously he doesn't realize what he has in her. So poor rejected Echo lives in the woods, pining and fading away until all that's left of her is her voice."

I bolted for the door, made it just outside before his hands gripped my legs and dragged me back in. My fingers clasped dirt and then nothing, helpless on the wooden floor.

"But I'm not going to let that happen to you," he whispered against my ear. "You see, I'm never going to let you go."

He released me, and I scrambled away. I huddled against the far wall, panting, while he considered me thoughtfully, not having broken a sweat. He closed the door, locking us inside.

"There's an alternate ending to the story. In this one, there was a god who fell in love with her. Echo, being rather cursed, rejects him. He gets so angry that he sends his followers. They tear her apart, Melody. Her pieces are scattered across the Earth."

I began to shake. "Is that what you did to Amanda?"

His face darkened, with pain not anger. "I would never have hurt her that way. And I'll never hurt you like that. You know that. You trusted me once."

"Never again," I spat.

He rubbed his forehead. "You'll need time to adjust, but I hate to see you like this. It may be hard to believe right now, but I do love you. If I didn't, I'd ship you back to Brendan well-used. That was the plan, but it changed pretty quickly once I met you. *You* changed my mind."

His expression softened, turned rueful. "You're the

whole package, smart and sexy, but your capacity for submission is a beautiful thing. So sweet, begging me to collar you." He held up a round silver collar.

This was what I wanted, dreamed of, but not like this. "Wait, please."

"This one's not leather. It's not coming off." He approached me.

I cringed away from him, holding my hands over my head.

"Shh," he soothed. "Don't look so terrified. It's unnerving. I'm going to take care of you. I'm going to hurt you, just a little, and then make you come. It's not a very scary proposition. What more do you want?"

"Freedom," I whispered.

"Freedom's an illusion. We all live in prisons of our own making. You picked this one. Kinky games in the city wasn't enough for you, but those men were too brutal. Little Goldilocks, walking into houses that aren't yours. This will be just right for you, Melody. I promise you that."

"Brendan will come find me." When had the man I feared become my potential savior?

"I don't think so. Not after the way we left things last time." His expression hardened. "Brendan didn't deserve you."

"This was only another one of your competitions." I was indignant. "He cheated on you with your girlfriend so now I'm just... just *payback*."

He chuckled softly. "Are you really upset because we fought over you? Or worried that I don't really care about you? What an insecure little girl. And look, I've told you I loved you and you haven't even said it back."

I stared at him mutinously. He'd be waiting a long time for that.

He softened. "Isn't this what you came here for? You wanted to be my girl, didn't you? My little subby?"

It seemed like a trick, surely it was. But I didn't really have a choice, and besides, it was the truth. I nodded.

"You want to be my sub, but now that you're here you're trying to set the terms." His expression was disapproving but indulgent. "No, subby. That's not how this works."

Sam held my hair aside with a tenderness that made me ache. I stayed still as he latched the collar around my neck and locked it. Overcome, I rested my cheek against his thigh. Was it true? I had come here to beg to be his sub. I had accepted that meant his authority over me, including how I lived, so what had really changed?

"That's my good girl," he said, stroking my hair.

"Master, you scared me." My voice trembled.

"I know." His thumb rubbed softly across the nape of my sneck, where the metal had warmed. He accepted the truth of my words without apology, but with comfort. *This is how it will be.*

I spilled tears of hope, unable to speak. He had promised to find the middle ground between play and horror, which was only everything I ever wanted. If I had come back here to find him pining for me, if he had sat down with a D/s contract, it would have been a dream. Instead I had come here to submit to his will, and this was it. I had come here to live under his care and control, and here I was.

A small, secret smile curved my lips. I looked down at the floor until I realized I didn't need to hide myself anymore. Turned my face to my master, I said, "I really do love you."

His eyes shone with possession and pride, and both feelings were reflected in my heart.

"I know, subby."

It was just like he promised. That night, and each one after that, he made me scream in pain and pleasure, and no one ever heard but him.

THE END

Thank you for reading Hear Me!

He horrified readers in Keep Me Safe and Trust in Me. Carlos is cruel, fearless, and irredeemable. Meet the woman who brings him to his knees in…

DON'T LET GO
coming 2013

ESCAPE

Included here is a bonus short story set in the same Dark Erotica world as Hear Me. The protagonist of this story was held captive in the same location. This was her escape.

PART ONE

Tiffany crawled over the damp concrete, ignoring the thick moldy grime beneath her hands and knees. Ignoring the way her torn skin and cramped muscles screamed at her to stop. None of it mattered when her life was at stake.

She would not cower. She would not break.

Even though her plan had worked, she was far from safe.

Safety had become a foreign concept exactly four weeks and three days ago. The cab she'd taken from the airport in Cancun had driven her, not to her hotel, but to a warehouse. From that moment, her life was over, but the pain never stopped.

After the four agonizing months of training, her captors were moving her and the other women. For two weeks she'd scraped and dug into the crumbly rock behind the metal toilet. It would never lead outside, but the hole was big enough for her to crawl into, and that's what she'd done as the men swept through the cells.

She'd mouthed off the night before and landed in the infirmary. Then she pretended to be fine, almost killing herself in the process, just so they'd release her back into her cell. She counted on the confusion about her actual location and the bustle of the transit.

Shockingly, it worked. They opened her door and glanced inside, and then moved on, leaving the door open.

She felt bad about the muffled cries of the other women, but she couldn't help them, not when she could barely help herself.

The whole thing had been a massive risk. Not only could they have found her, but they might have left the cell door locked. She'd have preferred to starve than go with them.

Tiffany huddled in the wall for hours after the last ringing footsteps had faded, sure that they would realize their mistake and come back for her. Or maybe they'd jump out at her from the walls once she emerged, laughing at the futility of her hope.

The halls were empty.

The sound of her ragged breathing and her skin dragging across the floor intruded on the stillness. She passed each cell as if she were still a prisoner – with her eyes straight ahead. She didn't want to see the small, barren cells with the thin, infested bedrolls. She didn't want to wonder about the dark spots staining the concrete.

Light leaked through the doorframe, blinding her. Sunlight so thick she thought she'd have been able to taste it if it weren't for the dank remains of stale bodily fluids lining her mouth.

Her body vibrated, as if her very bones felt the imminence of freedom. She had no idea where the warehouse was located or if she could survive long enough to find help, but even if she died, she'd die free.

The door creaked open at the touch of her fingertips. She managed to stand, slowly, shakily, and take a step out into the bright white ether. She savored the heat on her upturned face, the light wind that stroked her greasy hair. She'd made it.

The approaching rumble of a motor snapped her from euphoria. She darted for a copse of trees and made it inside just as an open topped jeep skidded in front of the building. Armed men burst from the vehicle before it was even fully stopped. Their guns were drawn as they entered the empty building.

Oh God. They must have realized she was missing and come back for her.

She didn't recognize the men or the vehicle, but that didn't mean anything at all. It would take them only minutes to realize she wasn't in the warehouse and then they would look outside.

Tiffany turned and crashed through the brush. Branches whipped at her legs and grabbed at her hair, but she tore through them like the hunted animal she was. Footsteps pounded behind her, giving her a last burst of speed.

"Wait! Stop," a voice called, but she would rather die.

PART TWO

The wood split beneath his axe with a satisfying crack. Alex wiped the stinging sweat from his eyes. He welcomed the small pain as his due and only wiped it so he wouldn't send the axe into his foot next. Although maybe that was what he needed. Maybe that would finally be enough.

But he knew it wouldn't.

There was no amount of pain he could inflict on himself that would equal what those women had gone through. Even if he tried, none of it would help them.

Nothing would help them. He'd seen that himself when he'd sat helplessly at Tiffany Scott's bedside. Even under heavy sedation she'd screamed and thrashed from the pain or the nightmares. He hadn't been able to do anything for her but badger and bully the doctor for higher doses until the man had threatened to have his visitation rights removed.

Naïve bastard that he'd been, Alex hadn't been

discouraged when he'd found her bruised and broken body at that hellhole. At least she was alive, he told himself. She would heal; he would make sure of it. Maybe that would help atone for what she'd gone through. Maybe if he helped her, it would begin to undo the damage.

Only fair, considering it was his fault she'd been abducted.

Her family had called in the missing persons report three weeks ago, frantic that their daughter, a grad student at NYU, hadn't called them since she'd landed in Cabo. It was supposed to be a vacation, a payoff for the years of grueling studies. One last hurrah before she officially entered the working world.

When the cops had been useless, her father had called him. He had done everything in his power, some of it questionable in its legality, to track her down and get her out, but none of it could assuage his guilt. He had used her, desperate to find the compound where the women were being held. Well, he'd found it all right.

Even though he'd been too late to protect her, Tiffany had found a way to escape. It should have been a happy ending. Certainly her family had cried happy tears and given him hugs, proclaiming him a hero. They didn't know what he had done, and he hadn't the courage to tell them. He didn't have the heart to break her father, because that's what the knowledge would have done.

The crunch of tires on gravel warned him of an intruder. He wiped his sweaty palms on his shirt and grabbed his gun from the table on his way out front.

He didn't anticipate trouble out here at his log cabin, but anyone who invaded his privacy was unwelcome. The green sedan—a rental—rolled to a halt. The door opened, and a woman stepped out. Alex blinked and wiped his eyes again, sure that the sweat and exertion had driven him to hallucinations.

She wasn't bloody or dirty the way he'd found her. Nor was she delirious and sweaty, caught in a nightmarish haze as she was when he'd sat beside her hospital bed those many weeks. Not even the laughing high school senior he'd glimpsed years ago.

This Tiffany was solemn, beautiful, and coming toward him. He'd hoped never to see her again, but he couldn't deny the lick of pleasure at the sight of her—strong and healthy. Maybe that was worst part, the things she stirred in him, dark and carnal.

"Are you going to use that, mister?" she asked.

He glanced at his hand, which had pointed the gun at the ground. "What the hell are you doing here?"

He didn't know why he was gruff with her. Sure, he didn't want people bugging him, but she didn't count. She could bother him any way she wanted and he would deserve it. The scary part, the part that made him scowl, was that he'd probably enjoy it anyway.

"I thought maybe we could talk." She bit her lip and her eyes flicked over to the leaning-sideways shanty that he now called home.

"Fine." He wanted to say no, to tell her to leave, but he couldn't. He led her inside without another word, shoving the gun onto a high shelf.

She sat on the lumpy futon carefully, as if it might give in any second. She probably didn't realize that he slept right there every night, and if his 200-pound frame couldn't do the thing in, her dainty self wasn't going to do the trick either.

She had definitely gained weight from the gaunt figure she'd been in the hospital bed, but she still looked too slim. Fragile. What was she doing driving through the mountains alone?

"What do you want?" he asked, too loudly.

His heart squeezed as she winced. He should be able to control himself better than that, but he'd misplaced his control after seeing her broken and begging and hadn't found it since.

She looked down at her folded hands then back up at him. "I need to thank you. My parents told me what you did for me. I know that you saved me. I also know you stayed beside me at the hospital before my parents got there." She frowned. "I can't remember most of it, but just knowing that someone cared enough to do that… well, it means a lot to me."

"I got paid for it," he said. "That's why I did it."

"You didn't get paid for sitting with me," she reminded him without missing a beat.

She misunderstood. She thought he meant her parents paying him to locate her. "That was just—" He cleared his throat against the thickness. "I'm the reason you were chosen."

"What are you talking about?"

"I'm a… well, I *was* a DEA agent, investigating some of the men involved. The trafficking thing wasn't our jurisdiction; we couldn't touch it." He shook his head, trying to explain how it had killed him to turn over the evidence to the FBI and watch them do nothing. "So I forced their hand: I planted evidence that the head office couldn't ignore. They green-lighted a raid, and so we went in."

"But I was already there. So you couldn't have had anything to do with me getting chosen." She looked perplexed, hopeful—and without an ounce of recognition.

"It was a trap. They were fucking with—" He caught himself. "Pardon me."

She gave him a small smile. "It's okay. My dad's a cop, so I'm used to it."

"That's right. Drug task force."

Her smile slipped. "How do you know that?"

"I worked with them. We do a lot of crossover stuff. Local intel contributing to the larger cases, that sort of thing. Your dad was part of a major bust two years ago, but I've been working with him since before then. I even met you once, when I happened to be in town for your big July 4th party. You were younger then, and I didn't have this." He waved at the beard that had grown in since he'd stopped giving a shit.

Abruptly, she stood and went to the door, but he got the idea that she needed air more than escape. "You think it's related," she said in a thin voice.

"I know it is. There was a note left in your hotel room saying so." There had been no written note, just a leather whip laced with blood, but she didn't need to know that detail.

"But if you and my dad helped catch the guys two years ago, then how…"

"These men are like insects. You destroy the hive and they just build another, only bigger. That combined agency taskforce caught the low-hanging fruit, while everyone important got away. This time was even worse. Between the FBI blocking us and the usual red tape, they couldn't get permission for a raid." He shook his head, pushing away all the illegal shit he'd pulled just to get her location, trying to forget the pain of arriving there only to find it empty. Luckily he'd had some basic skills in tracking and had found the trail of a single person, barefoot—her.

"If this is all true, then why didn't my father tell me?"

"He doesn't know. That was years ago, there was no reason to link the two except for the note. Then you were free and he needed to be there to help you heal. It's up to you, but I'd prefer you don't tell him. The guilt…" It was like ice, cutting him open and keeping him that way, frozen. But how could he complain to her after what she had been through? He couldn't. "…it wouldn't be good for him."

Her eyes narrowed, as if maybe she heard thoughts left unspoken. "It wasn't his fault. Or yours. You were just doing your job. No." She put a hand to her forehead, the gesture at once emphasizing her fragility and underscoring her strength. "You were doing the right thing. I would never wish for someone to be stuck there, not if there was a chance of you getting them free. You saved those women before. You saved *me*."

Her unbending belief in him threatened to undo him. "If I had been there in time... If I had known..." He'd been too late, but like a miracle, she stood before him, patiently waiting for his answer. "I saw what they did to you and how you couldn't sleep, refused to eat."

The bright sheen of tears covered her eyes, but still she went on. "I would be dead now if not for you."

"That's right," he said, willing to lay everything out if she'd only understand. "You're alive now because of me. You asked me...you begged me to let you die. To help you do it while you were trapped in that hospital room, but I couldn't. That was my raid, my responsibility, and you were targeted as a result of that. I wanted to be a fucking savior, and I was willing to let you suffer to accomplish it."

His voice was hoarse by the time he finished. The words flayed him in a way that months of self-enforced exile and backbreaking physical labor never had. The guilt taunted him. She had been out there, alive and suffering.

Then Tiffany was standing in front of him, her cheeks wet with tears, but her eyes focused. "I'm glad you didn't help me do that," she said fiercely. "I *am* better. Not completely and probably I never will be, but I'm alive. I'm free. Maybe I had my weak moments, but I'm even more grateful now that you were there to keep me from letting them win."

She took his hands, her touch warm and soothing. "You did the right thing."

The crack in his guilt wound its way through his body, just that small sliver allowing him to see light again, to imagine a future. She was so strong to have survived, to have escaped. Strong enough to come and break him out of his own self-imposed prison. He was the one in awe. He looked down at their linked hands and gently squeezed. *Thank you.*

THE END

Thank you for reading Hear Me!

TRUST IN ME

Mia longs for the daily torture to end, but one last task keeps her holding on. In a betrayal of the crime lord who pulled her from the gutter, she'll free the shipment of human cargo, and if she's lucky, die in the process. The alternative is unfathomable, even to a woman well-versed in erotic torture. But luck abandons her yet again when she meets the security expert in charge of the shipment and finds herself face to face with her childhood crush. The man she once begged for help. The man who failed her.

Tyler Martinez is an undercover FBI agent with one chance to right the wrongs of his past. Thrust deep into the seedy world of human trafficking, he must put aside his guilt over abandoning Mia all those years ago in order to save her now.

"Dark, disturbing, haunting, and beautiful, Skye Warren will take you into the depths of depravity but bring you home, safe in the end."

- Kitty Thomas, author of Comfort Food

First chapter of TRUST IN ME:

"Come, bitch."

His words dragged my body across the floor, invisible chains. I hated him for calling me that way. I hated myself more for going to him. And I went the way I knew he wanted me to—crawling. A layer of grime covered the concrete floor of the warehouse, but it was only fitting to crawl through muck. This whole game was dirty, and so was I.

Carlos looked down at me from his seat with a half-smile. The guy next to him was speaking in low, urgent tones, but I had his attention.

Other whores might try coy smiles or a flash of cleavage, but if you really knew El Jefe—and, unfortunately, I did—then you knew all you had to do was drop to his feet. I knew what he wanted and how he liked it, knowledge born of years of training. As long as I behaved, he wouldn't kill me. I craved the release of death, but I was too well trained to earn it.

I reached his leather shoes and waited. The same Italian leather shoes that had kicked me only recently, but they weren't a danger to me now. Carlos didn't like to get too messy when he had guests. Even though I didn't like performing, I could be glad this new guy was around today. Then again, I'd probably have to service him next.

Carlos unzipped his pants.

The guy sucked in a quiet breath, as if we'd shocked him.

That wouldn't stop Carlos. He wasn't an

127

exhibitionist. He was a sadist, and the only thing better than causing someone physical pain was causing emotional discomfort. Every pinch was designed to humiliate, every blow to subjugate. *You're not worthy,* they said, and I lapped up every blow to my shrunken ego like the masochist I'd learned to be.

Eagerly, I leaned forward and sucked the head of his cock with my mouth. Eager because delays were only an excuse to punish me later, and Carlos was nothing if not creative, and extreme, in his punishments. The whips, the knives, the *cage.* I shuddered.

His cock was musky today, but not urine-tinged—I could be thankful for that, too. Finding things to be thankful for kept me sane. It could always be worse. It had been.

I worked my tongue in a swirl and laved under the tip of his cock. Carlos grunted.

It was almost funny, the way the guy next to him stuttered a few starts, as if unsure if he should continue talking to the infamous *El Jefe* while he was getting his dick sucked. I hadn't gotten a good look at the guy, just a brief glimpse of jeans and a black t-shirt. Mostly I noticed a big, strong male body. That was enough. Maybe some girls got turned on. I just got scared. It wasn't about weakness or strength. This was pure survival instinct.

"Go on, Martinez," Carlos said gruffly. "Continue."

Martinez started talking again, something about deliveries and security. Carlos put his hands over my ears. Not so I couldn't hear the conversation. He never worried about trusting me because he didn't think I was smart enough to do anything about it. That was my one victory, however small.

No, his hands over my ears were a warning. If I didn't do it on my own, he'd shove my face down so I couldn't breathe. I could deep throat before I came here, but two years with Carlos had beaten the skill right out of me. He didn't train me to do better, he beat me to do worse, until my nerves manifested in performance that could be punished. He loved to hold my face down so I couldn't breathe, until even a shallow blowjob filled me with panic.

I pushed my head down, forcing his cock to slide along my tongue and sink deep in my throat. *Breathe,* I told myself firmly, *and whatever you do, don't gag.* Gagging didn't make him angry, it made him horny. The sadistic kind of horny that led to worse things.

I pulled back. His fingers tightened in my hair, not letting me go too far. Then I plunged down again. And again. Over and over I took him deep in my throat, still breathing, not gagging. So far, so good.

Martinez, though—damn. I glanced up, trying to see the man, but Carlos's arm blocked my view. All I could see was a strong jaw obscured by a few days' scruff and a low-pulled cap. It couldn't be him. Martinez was a common enough name. He was long gone, but the memories rattled in their cage.

Hey, little girl. Whatcha doing out here?

Nothin'.

You should do nothin' inside then. It's not safe out here.

The man in my memories hadn't known it wasn't safe inside either. Or maybe he had known, but

129

pretended he didn't. He wouldn't have been the only one to turn away. The long-buried memories escaped their tight confines, flooding my mind. They had no place in my life now. Every whore had a sob story, but no one wanted to think about it—least of all the whore.

Maybe Carlos could tell I was distracted because he clamped his hand behind my head and shoved it all the way down. His cock popped into my throat with a sickening gurgle. I worked at a swallow, but I couldn't help it—I gagged. Panic swept over me, tossing me, drowning me. *Can't breathe, let me go.*

I forced my arms to remain by my sides, where he wanted them. I'd rather pass out than suffer a punishment. At least, my mind knew that. My body squirmed and jerked in tiny pleas for mercy. Finally, thankfully, he pulled back my head just enough to pop his cock out of my throat. I sucked in deep breaths through my nose—grateful, so grateful—until he shoved it back in again. It shouldn't have been a surprise, but somehow it was, every time. The ache, the burn, the horror that I'd let this happen to me yet again.

His cock filled my awareness, until all I smelled or felt or could think of was the thick flesh in my mouth. When it was in, I was in pain, I couldn't breathe, I must not move. When it was out, the sweet rush of air breathed consciousness back into me.

His movements became jerky. His hand tightened painfully in my hair. I imagined his face pale and tight as it was right before he came, but my nose was buried in his crotch and my eyes were full of tears.

He yanked my head far enough back that only the tip

of his cock was in before he spewed his load into my mouth. I knew he wanted me to get the full impact of the spray, the full salty flavor of his come that wouldn't have happened if he'd been deep. Even swallowing was degrading, a voluntary act.

Unlike other men I'd seen, and the few I'd serviced, Carlos barely ever made a sound when he came. Mostly he was silent, tense and contained even in his crisis. When he released me, I staggered back onto the floor. He wouldn't hurt me, not so soon after he'd come, so I lay there, sprawled and heaving, waiting for my eyes to dry and my breath to catch.

When the shadowed office came into focus, I looked away from the sight of Carlos tucking himself into his pants and peeked at the other guy. Martinez. Light brown hair, almost a sandy blond that belied his surname, and a strong jaw. He looked up at me. Blue eyes seared mine like a blinding summer sun.

Oh God. I knew him. It wasn't a coincidence. He was *my* Martinez, though the ownership was only in my delusions. Tyler Martinez, my childhood neighbor, the golden boy of the *barrio.* I'd had a massive crush on him. He'd barely noticed me, though in his defense, he was older than me, which was a big deal when I was twelve and he was eighteen. Then he'd left for the military, I heard, and I never saw him again. Until now.

Those blue eyes widened as he looked at me, mirroring my own shock. His lips formed my name, *Mia,* but thank God, no sound emerged. I couldn't believe he recognized me. It had been—what?—ten years. I couldn't believe he even remembered me.

131

I must look different, all grown up. And—oh God—I'd just sucked a guy off in front of him. Not just any guy, a crime boss with a penchant for whores. Tyler knew who I was, what I was. My stomach knotted, trying to turn my body inside out. I wanted to die. My self-hatred, which I would have thought peaked years ago, climbed another notch. Bad enough that this was my life, bad enough this had always been my life, but for him to know, for him to have seen me this way, was too much.

"Here, cunt, show our new friend some hospitality," Carlos said.

No. I don't want to. That thought distracted me for a second. Since when did I say no, even in my mind? Somewhere deep inside, did I still think I had the right?

I met Tyler's gaze again and was snapped back to reality. The life where, no, I didn't have a choice. And where, worst of all, he looked chagrined by the thought of a blowjob from me. More than that, he looked disgusted, leaning away, not meeting my eyes. Jesus, there was a blow to the self-esteem I didn't even know I had. I deserved his revulsion. I knew that better than him, but it hurt to see the eyes I had once longed for, dreamed of, judging my scantily clad body.

Pain slammed through my side. I gasped for air. Those boots again. Damn, I hadn't been watching. Too distracted. "Come on," Carlos was saying, "what's taking you so long, you stupid bitch?"

Every cell of my body screamed to run. I would rather die, rather suffer any punishment, than touch Tyler as a whore. I'd gladly pleasure him of my own free will, but not like this. Tears filled my eyes. At least Carlos would think they were from the pain. I'd never been able to hold them back, which was probably the reason why I was Carlos's favorite girl. His only girl.

I would have to comply. Even if I decided to leave for good, I'd have to wait and do it when I was alone. Plan an escape. If I balked now, Carlos would just beat the shit out of me until I obeyed. Or until I died. Besides, I had a purpose here. If I could help a single girl escape this, it was worth it. My dignity had dried up years ago, but other women still had a chance.

With my mouth filled with the bitter taste of Carlos's semen and my own self-loathing, I shuffled toward Tyler. He shifted on the seat as I approached. I knew he didn't want this. It was clear in his eyes, his posture, as if I was attacking him and he was trapped. How ironic.

I almost wanted Tyler to refuse. Almost.

If he refused me, Carlos would make me pay the price, and it would be dear. Which would I prefer, to make myself a whore of my childhood crush or to suffer unspeakable pain?

But it wasn't my choice to make after all, because Tyler said, "Stop."

I froze, waiting for it, hoping, dreading.

"You don't like her?" Carlos asked. His voice held a warning note, not to Tyler, but to me. "Let us seal our partnership. I can bring in another girl if this one doesn't please you."

"No," Tyler said, his voice strangled. "I…like her. She's good. I was just thinking I wanted more time with her, maybe a room."

My breath caught. Mostly I hated the idea. But a small part of me, the part of me that was still a childish little girl and hopeful, loved it. As if this could be the erotic coupling of my dreams, a shiny peel to disguise the rotting core of human slavery.

"Ah, privacy," Carlos mused. "You'd like to play with her alone."

We waited. I didn't know what Tyler's agenda was, whether he truly wanted me or if it was just a ploy to get out of a blowjob from a dirty whore, but I held my breath for the verdict.

"That is fine," Carlos said lightly, as if he hadn't just answered my prayers and doomed me at the same time.

Tyler's breath released along with mine.

"Take him to my bedroom," Carlos said. "Tyler is my good friend, so please him well." *Or else.*

I stood up and straightened my skimpy halter and short skirt, as if I had any dignity left, and led Tyler from the room. Neither of us spoke as we moved through the barren halls. Not even as we passed a couple of the men, who leered but knew better than to mess with me when I had Tyler at my side.

Once inside Carlos's room, I studied it through Tyler's eyes. Shiny surfaces and gaudy mirrors left no doubt as to what sort of acts they normally reflected. The leather wall paneling and black silk sheets cinched the deal—this room was for sex.

Tyler whirled on me. I could tell he was going to say something, ask something, so I kissed him. It was only to stop him, but I enjoyed myself anyway. Be thankful where you can, that was my motto, and I was thankful for this. His lips were soft and warm, and shockingly, he responded to my kiss, pressing his lips back and tangling his tongue with mine. He wasn't chilly or slimy. He didn't taste bad.

When we parted, we were both panting. With my lips only an inch from his, I breathed, "There's cameras."

His eyes widened for a second, then he nodded slightly. His arms came around me and pulled my body into his. He understood. Don't act like we know each other, don't say anything incriminating. From the moment we'd pretended not to know each other, it was me and Tyler against Carlos.

How had he come to work with Carlos? How had he ended up back in the old neighborhood? I had imagined him somewhere with a great family and a good job. I didn't like that he was back here in Shitsville, mixed up with dangerous people.

"So Carlos just gives his girlfriend to anyone who asks?" he asked in a low tone.

From somewhere deep I pulled a careless laugh. "I'm not his girlfriend."

He raised one eyebrow. "That's not how it looked to me."

God, the innocence. He really wasn't cut out to be working with a guy like Carlos. "I'm whatever he tells me to be," I said, infusing myself with a sexiness I didn't feel. "I'm a whore."

Tyler's eyes darkened. "Why?"

"A girl's gotta eat," I said lightly. It wasn't even a lie. That had been the reason once. I stroked a finger down my neck because it seemed like something a whore would do, and because I wanted to.

His fingertips tightened on my hips, and he shook me slightly. "Damn it, Mia."

I sharpened my gaze in warning.

"Isn't that what you said your name was?" he murmured.

Then he kissed me. It was an act, like my kiss had been, but just as quickly it became real. He tasted me, caressed me, and I'd never had it like this. I'd never been kissed by a man who treated me gently, who knew who I was, and at least for the moment, wanted me anyway. I'd never been kissed by a man I liked. I'd never liked a man that wasn't Tyler. I didn't deserve it but I took it anyway, which made me just as bad as Carlos.

"How long do we have?" he asked between breaths.

"As long as you want," came the automatic reply.

He nipped at my lips. Not the right answer.

"Maybe an hour," I whispered. Any longer and Carlos would get anxious. Much less and he'd know I hadn't properly pleased Tyler. "Are you going to…?" *Fuck me.*

"I don't know," he muttered. "I wasn't counting on cameras. What happens if we just kiss? Make out?"

Pain. Tears. Blood. "Nothing," I said. "Do what you want."

He scowled.

I widened my eyes. "What?"

"You're not as good a liar as you think you are. What happens if we don't fuck?" he asked.

His voice held a command, and that, at least, I was used to. Damn. I didn't know if I could trust this guy, but somewhere deep inside I already did.

"I'll get in trouble." I shook my head to show him it didn't matter. The last thing I wanted to do was pressure him into sex.

"What kind of trouble?" he asked. When I didn't answer, he pulled me tighter against him. I went limp, a reflex. "What happens when you get in trouble?"

My throat tightened. I couldn't tell him, couldn't explain about the pain. The terror, the agony.

"Christ," he said. "Tell me."

I shook my head. "It's nothing." *It's everything. Please, just fuck me.*

"If he hurts you then why…?"

I knew what he'd meant to say. Why did I stay, then? The irony was that I had the same question for him. Working for a guy like Carlos had "bad idea" written all over it. Why would anyone want to stay in this shithole if he had the option to leave? But both of us were here. The better question was, what was holding us prisoners?

Trust in Me is available at Amazon.com, BarnesandNoble.com, AllRomanceEbooks.com and Kobo.com.

Other Books by Skye Warren

Wanderlust
Below the Belt

Dark Erotica Series
Keep Me Safe
Trust in Me
Hear Me
Don't Let Go

The Beauty Series
Beauty Touched the Beast
Beneath the Beauty
Broken Beauty
Beauty Becomes You

Fem Dom Series
Sweetest Mistress
Cherry On Top (coming 2014)

Dystopia Series
Leashed
Caged

ABOUT THE AUTHOR

Skye Warren writes unapologetic erotica, including power play or erotic pain and sometimes dubious consent. There's struggle in the sex. There's pain in the relationships. Her books are raw, sexual and perversely romantic.

Visit Skye's website for her current booklist:
skyewarren.com

Follow Skye Warren on Twitter:
@skye_warren

Find her on Facebook:
facebook.com/skyewarren

16218823R00092

Made in the USA
San Bernardino, CA
24 October 2014